Praise for *Mostly White*

"Alison Hart's debut novel, *Mostly White*, spans five generations and about one hundred years in a family with American Indian, African American, and Irish roots. It is a uniquely American story showing how people from the cultures and traditions of three continents found themselves together in the North American wilderness, sometimes in conflict and misunderstanding but other times in cooperation and love. Their mixed-race descendants are ordinary yet courageous people who survive against the terrible odds imposed by racism and poverty to pass both sorrow and inner strength down to their children and grandchildren. Hart has written a great American epic, which should be read and discussed for many generations to come."

—**Lucille Lang Day, author of *Married at Fourteen* and *Becoming an Ancestor***

"In a world clamoring for diverse voices and characters in whom readers can see themselves, as well as learn about people different from themselves, Alison Hart's *Mostly White* is a beacon. Through the story of four generations of women, from a mixed-race Native and African American family, our eyes and hearts are opened to a world we may not know, but should."

—**Andrew Weiner, Abrams Books**

"The trickle-down effect of genocidal practices and values—many of you have forgotten but our souls bear the costs of your purposely lost memories. Here are some of those soul stories . . . read and weep for us all. Thank you, Alison, for remembering the ancestors."

—**Abby Abinanti, Yurok, Chief Judge of the Yurok Tribal Court**

"There is a genius of the heart, as well as the mind, and this book gives profound evidence that the author possesses both in abundance . . . Ms. Hart is not only keeping the faith, but she is passing it on to anyone who shares the epic heart-rending and soul-lifting experience of this book . . . a stunning achievement."

—Roberta Lee Tennant, Falcon Books

"The immediate trust and bond of spirit meets the eruption of soul-searching prose, poetry, and the history of us all! Powerful and dangerous because these women are so real!"

—Jerry Thompson, co-editor of *Oakland Noir* and *Berkeley Noir*, and co-owner of Owl & Company Bookshop, Oakland, CA

MOSTLY WHITE

MOSTLY WHITE

A novel
by Alison Hart

TORREY HOUSE PRESS

SALT LAKE CITY • TORREY

First Torrey House Press Edition, November 2018
Copyright © 2018 by Alison Hart

Published by Torrey House Press
Salt Lake City, Utah
www.torreyhouse.org

MIX
Paper from
responsible sources

FSC
www.fsc.org   FSC® C011935

International Standard Book Number: 978-1-937226-95-4
E-book ISBN: 978-1937226-99-2
Library of Congress Control Number: 2018932561

Cover design by Kathleen Metcalf
Interior design by Rachel Davis
Distributed to the trade by Consortium Book Sales and Distribution

For my son, Luis

won't you celebrate with me

won't you celebrate with me
what i have shaped into
a kind of life?
born in babylon
both nonwhite and woman
what did i see to be except myself?
i made it up
here on this bridge between
starshine and clay,
my one hand holding tight
my other hand; come celebrate
with me that everyday
something has tried to kill me
and has failed.

—Lucille Clifton, *The Book of Light*

PART I

In 1879, the Bureau of Indian Affairs established a law that forced all Indian children to go to school. Many children were removed from their families and sent to residential schools. These schools were run by religious groups and funded by the Federal Government.

ELLA

I *didn't know how to stop hatred from entering my body. It was words looks thoughts energy swirling around me—and it got in effortlessly, I an open field became a deposit for other people's waste*
    receptacle
    My mother couldn't stop it; she didn't know how and most of the time she didn't see it—she was wrapped up in some other world creating her own sanity. I didn't know it was entering my body—filling my cells with aversion I accepted like the images of white blue-eyed blond-haired children on the TV screen reflecting what I would never be, but thought I was or should be—
    Hatred entered my brain firing off neurons a pattern now ancient etched into my skull.
    It was familiar, my body knew it somehow, it was already there so it must belong there. Soon I grew a cannonball heart of self-hatred, shame, and doubt all based on someone else's contempt for others, someone else's need for dominance—
    someone else's inner fear.
    I was floating in the world with this heartache cannonball trying to find a place to land. I didn't understand where it came from, all I knew was that I'd find myself on the floor weeping, trying to push something out out out—
    or maybe it was like being haunted and having no words or

images to name an experience of utter devastation.
    This is how I floated through the world, that is, until I landed
    I landed and found
                roots.

EMMA

Washington County, Maine
1890

SNAKE

They beat me, I'll tell you that's what they did, at that school, they beat me, huh! School! If I spoke my language oooooh—those nuns would get so mad called it the devil's language and Sister Anne, oh she'd get out the switch—
Everyone's eyes in the class widen—turn to me.

I didn't care I was tough huh, I was too tough for them, already eleven, they beat me and I didn't cry. Tried to beat the Indian out of me, only good Indian is dead Indian, kill the savage kill the savage save the man . . .

Take me to the front of the class and with that switch smack smack smack until I bled. They couldn't get to me I made myself real small so small no one could get to me it wasn't me they were beating they couldn't get to me.

"That's what any one of you will get if you speak the devil's language in here." Sister Anne props the switch by her desk. Silence in room—I am a lump on the floor. My brother, he is the only one that can see me that small pebble I've become. Joe wipes his eyes.

Joe don't cry, silly Joe—you know she didn't get to me no—you know that little Joe, little Joe—

My head is facedown. I can see the crack in the floorboards, smells like dust. Cold dust.

"Get up, you little nigger savage!" She sounds like a snake hissing.

Sssssssssssssssssavage

"I said get up!"

I get up hissing Sssssssssssssssssssssssssssssssss she is a snake Ssssssssssssssss I stamp my foot bent low. They know—the class knows, they want to join the dance, like we did back home, they shift in their chairs—

Sssssssssssssssssssssssss I move around the room, Sister Anne shouts, "You come here, you little savage!"

Sssssssssssssssssssss I swerve past her, in between desks Sssssssssssssssssss I head towards the door, the open door. Why aren't the children holding my hands, so we can coil, coil up like a snake? I smell sage. A rattle shakes. I go towards the door.

"You come here right now!" She gets the switch, stomps towards me, I turn towards the door, the children bang on desks—the beat—beat of the drum—the beat. Sister Anne catches me, grips my arm. Loud footsteps, Sister Dorothy comes. "What is going on?"

"Quick, get her—she's speaking the devil's language."

"Devil's language, is she?" Sister Dorothy clenches my arm—I'm bent down, foot stamping, the children banging the desks—pulse of the drum.

She holds me down one of them I don't know who, I feel the switch over and over again—

Sssssssssssssssssss I say Ssssssssssssssssssss—

They take me to the closet—

Sssssssssssssssssss

Throw me in the closet. Now I am in darkness. I can still hear the faint sound of the children beating their desks—the drum.

"It's that nigger Indian again, is it?" Sister Dorothy says.

"The devil's in her, devil's in her blood, that one." Sister Anne spits out her words like venom.

"Let's see if this won't help." A lock clicks.

"Keep her in for a good time this time."

"Yes, Sister Dorothy, yes."

"Now tend to your class before the others go on the warpath."

"Yes, Sister Dorothy." Her footsteps fade off.

I don't know how long they locked me in there that closet—days I don't know sunrise sunset sunrise? I don't know. I soiled myself plenty. Joe and the rest of them beating their desks, some medicine. Back stings, back of my dress sticky—too much blood.

A click, the lock opens, light shoots to my eyes. "You filthy beast!" Sister Anne yanks me. I don't resist.

"Had to make a mess in there, did you?" She pulls my hair.

"Get those clothes off!" I don't move.

"You filthy savage, get them off!" She rips the dress off me, it tears skin off my back. I don't move. I feel blood trickle down my legs—she pulls me by the hair.

"Get in!" She puts me in big metal basin pours cold water on me—she scrubs so hard my skin red red water red. "That will teach you to speak the devil's language in the Lord's house, this will teach you!"

They scrubbed me and Joe scrubbed so hard Joe cried and cut our hair short. Fell to ground in clumps—I wanted to scoop it up, I did from those mean Sisters, scoop it up and put it back on my head. Burned our clothes. Gave us new clothes white scratchy, smelled funny not soft like deer or sealskin. Scratchy. Maybe they burned our hair with the clothes. Spirit soaring to the sky.

How long Joe and I been here? One moon? Came to our house they did, came rounded up all of us—me my brother Joe, we didn't have a lot to eat, not much those agents handed out. We poor Papa trying to grow garden—hard soil tough soil. Agent bring food. Mama died, she died of coughing sickness, my mama black not Indian, she learned from Papa and his people. Aunt Julia brought my mama to us for Papa's medicine.

Aunt Julia is black too, my papa healed my mama, but the sickness came back and took her. Papa fish, Papa hunt bring food when he can. Papa face sad since Mama died coughing disease his eyes far away like he's in some other world.

Papa try and stop men from taking us. Joe and I were playing in yard—they came and took us.

"This one's dark." He holds my arms hard. "Real dark Indian." Joe cries, trying to get away from other man's arms. They drag us to cart, howls of children crying—Papa runs out of house.

"Where you taking my children?"

Agent says, "All Indian children got to go to school."

"Where you taking them?" Papa jumps on one of them like a bear the other agent raises his stick and beats Papa, beat him till I can't see Papa move—just lump on ground. Papa, please get up please please get up. Last time I seen of Papa—on the ground.

Me and Joe huddle in dark all children weeping sound of horse hooves on ground crack of whip. Time to civilize and educate Indians the agent said, Joe crying I'm holding him. We get to school the place we would unlearn our savage ways. They stripped us scrubbed us cut our hair. Any time anyone speak Passamaquoddy smack of hand or lash with switch. We learn to speak without speaking.

"Get up and go to morning prayers!" Sister Anne commands. She shakes me—I'm cold—floor cold on my feet. I walk to church, all brown heads bowed in white clothing kneeling—

"Our Father who art in heaven hallow be thy name." I kneel by Joe—Joe frowns. "Thy Kingdom come thy will be done." I pinch his leg, he shoots a glance, I smile.

After Mass, breakfast. I'm so hungry one bowl of something lumpy I eat it anyways—always hungry at this place. We march in one at a time Sister Anne tapping switch in her hand—my back throbs.

I am dazed in class words tumble out of Sister Anne's mouth

like gurgling brook. I can't make sense of it. Am I here? Or my spirit somewhere else, disappeared through closet floorboards.

Joe has rabbit fear in his eyes. I can't reach him. Chore time, scrubbing floor, sweeping, dusting, my body does it. Where am I?

Lunch time. Some watery soup, my body eats it the children scared to talk to me afraid of beatings. Back to class more gurgling brook talk. More chores. Sister Anne's piercing voice:

"Sweep that dirt in a pile first then sweep it in the dust pan. Don't you know how to sweep a floor?"

My body follows commands, back to dinner, some stew. Nighttime prayers, we kneel beside bed all girls, booming voice of the Father we try to mimic his words as he walks by our beds, he stops at mine. Will I die? Will I die and go to hell? Father stares at me with steel blue eyes—my spine shivers.

I am awake or asleep, someone heavy on me, it's dark—

"You—you seductress I know what you want." The Father whispers in my ear hand over my mouth. His face is red, hair white like snow. He lifts up blanket something hard enter me he thrusts up and down up and down pain stabbing through my body—

"This is what happens to sinners!" The Father's thrusts become harder, faster—

Am I dead? Did I go to hell? Is this hell? Joe Joe where are you—his scared rabbit eyes was his warning. Pierce sharpness over and over—

I am dead, am I? I smell sweetgrass the kind my mother used to hang.

Something sticky wet down my legs.

"You savage seductress you made me do it."

He leaves. I am frozen I am in the hell they speak of.

Morning prayer. Hard to walk. My spirit gone I am just body. We kneel say morning prayer.

"Our Father who art in heaven hallow be thy name—"
insides ache—
"Thy Kingdom come thy will be done—"
I am just a body—
"on earth as it is in heaven. Give us this day our daily
bread—"
My spirit
"and forgive us our trespasses—"
Where are you?
"As we forgive those who trespass against us—"
Where are you?
"And lead us not into temptation but deliver us from
evil—"
I must get you
"For thine is the Kingdom the power the glory—"
back!
"forever and ever Amen."
The Father closes the bible and leaves, Sister Anne rushes
us to breakfast.
"Joe," I whisper to him, "Joe, my spirit gone I must find it
today at lesson follow me."
Joe nods his head, Sister Anne shoves me away from him
back in line for breakfast.

Sunlight through window, door creak open, calls me to find
my spirit. Sister Anne bounces switch in her hand all eyes on
switch—except me. My eyes on door. She commands us to copy
letters heads bent over slates, she walks up and down the aisle
past me, past Joe.
My spirit calls me.
I take Joe's hand run towards door her back is to us—we
run—me and Joe run—past the pasture, the outhouse into the
woods—warning bells ring—I hold tight to Joe. Someone is
behind us, Joe trips—lets go—he screams they get him—I run,

I shout, "Joe, Joe!"

"Run big sister run!" he cries.

"I will come back for you." I dash into trees I can't turn back—my spirit calls—so fast I run I run until it's dark. I run until I can't see.

They tie you up to a tree and leave you there oh Joe, Joe. The last one that tried to run, they caught and tied him to a tree. We couldn't talk to him, or give him food or water, his eyes, lifeless, until he couldn't stand no more. I rock back and forth under a tree, I rock, the owl hoots, tears stream down for Joe, I rock, listen for spirit.

BIRD MAN

Coo of dove calls me, time to keep moving. Father Sun shines through green leaves of trees. My stomach rumbles for food, I spot pink flowers ahead of me. My mama and aunties showed me how to dig up roots and find the nuts. I get a stick and dig out the thickest root of the vine, pull it hard and out comes a necklace of round nuts. I brush them off, eat half and save the rest. I run to tall reeds of grass, sunlight bounces off pointed edges, smell water. Come to edge of riverbank and wait in sunlight, maybe spirit is in water, I drink from it, wait for river to bring my spirit back.

I lay back on the rock, river rushes past me. The warmth of stone heals my back, still feel Sister Anne's switch. I drift in dreamland—

Little one, remember the story of Bear Island. We are the bear clan. My mother Sophia, a bear medicine woman, your grandmother. She had healing powers to cure ill, foraged forests for plants and herbs. White man disease came too strong—the pox. Came to Bear Island—whole island suffered, the wails echoed at night, wolves across the bay answered back. My mother tried, used herbs for my father Joseph, my brothers, sisters, aunts, uncles—

pox took them. *We went to bring them to rest with ancestors, to the mainland. We carry dead in a canoe heading toward mainland, they shoot arrows at us, forcing us to go back. They didn't want the pox. My mother set the camp on fire, we left at night in a canoe, wolves howling, people howling, owls hooting—there was no peace that night.*

Long journey, yes it was, all night gliding down the river, stars leading the way. Father Sun rises, on the shore, my mother offers tobacco. I carefully step out of the canoe and join her, facing the four directions. We walk in silence through the forest. My mother shows me what herbs and roots to pick. I eat berries and my mother fasts, so she can be hollow like a drum to receive the spirit. She thanks the plants as we go. My moccasins worn, I keep going. The cries of the people and the wolf howls haunt me, I keep going. Grandmother Moon lights our way to the bay. I gather branches for the fire. I sleep curled in my mother's lap.

Father Sun peeks through the trees. We walk to the river, to the stones. Father Sun rises, the stones light up and pictures appear. The spirit rocks speak to my mother. She sits and prays listening for the song of our ancestors, waiting for the medicine. I don't speak—the images speak to me: bird men flying, a woman with two dogs her arms raised to the sky world, a salamander from under the earth world, all carved in stone. I wait until sun shifts across the sky and magic pictures disappear. Across the bay a mother bear wades in the river with her cubs, she catches a salmon. My mother speaks to the bear. The fish squirms in the bear's mouth. She heads into the forest with her little ones behind her.

"Judah," my mother says, "come." I follow her into the woods and help her strip birch bark off the birch trees. We wind the birch around a stick and tie it, to save for later to catch salmon. We rest before sundown, head back to the cove—the pictures light up one last time, the message from our ancestors fading with the light. We light the birch torch. My mother holds the torch over the water, I take out my knife waiting for the fish. Something in the water

flutters towards the light, I stab the fish, my mother says a prayer. It wriggles as we carry it to shore. We thank the salmon. I light a fire and we cook the fish, my mother finally eats, and what we don't eat, we give back to the river.

I awake to my mother talking with a deer, we follow it through the forest, back to our canoe. My mother lights sage, offers tobacco, giving thanks to great spirit mystery. And that's how we came here little one, your grandmother, bear medicine woman, from Bear Island. Always remember, we belong to the land.

"Papa." I call for him. I lift my head, he's not here. It was the stone, he spoke to me through the stone.

"I first set my eyes on sweet Molly Malone."

A voice rises from the river like some great bird. A man sings alone in canoe.

"As she wheeled her wheelbarrow
through streets broad and narrow
crying cockles and mussels
alive alive-oh!"

I want his canoe. I start throwing rocks at this Bird Man, big rocks—

"Alive alive-oh—" He stops singing, and frowns. I hide behind stone and throw one smack on back of his head—that stops his singing—

"Who's there?" he hollers, he sees me, rock in hand. I keep throwing them, pelting him. He paddles canoe to shore, I dart into tall reeds.

"Why are you throwing stones at me, lass? Is my singing that bad?"

I throw another one, it hits his leg, he winces. He has boots on, is white man with a funny way to speak. I throw another stone at him—he rushes towards me and I run to his canoe, he runs after me and catches me like I'm a fish—caught in his net arms. I struggle, kick, he strong, he got me.

"Okay, lass, you want to go in the canoe, let's go in the canoe." He picks me up, drops me in, ties my hands behind me and paddles down the river. He starts singing again: *"Alive alive-oh, oh Alive alive-oh—crying cockles and mussels alive alive-oh."*

I am a fish trapped—

"What, you're angry because you got no stones to throw?" He takes a drink from a bottle, it shines and reflects the sun—

"Alive-alive-oh, oh Alive-Alive Oh—crying cockles and mussels alive alive-oh."

Where are you, spirit? I am fish now caught waiting for you. This strange man won't stop singing. Joe, where is Joe? Father's blue eyes, Sister Anne's switch, the smell of the floorboards—I don't know it but I'm shaking, shaking and writhing about like a fish out of water. The singing man tries to stop me: "There, there, have some of this to calm you down."

He offers me the bottle, I take it. I drink it, tastes awful. I drink more, my head feels light, my body warm—oh spirit have I found you?

Where am I? Am I dead? Owl's omen come true? Where's Joe? Where's Joe? I jump out of bed running into other room—

"Joe! Joe!" There are many barrels big, and bottles empty like the one in the canoe. Where is that strange Bird Man? Did he bring me here? I turn quick, a bottle crashes. Bird Man walks in smoking a pipe.

"What's all the ruckus in here? Someone finally woke up?"

"Joe! Joe!" I shout—

"There's no Joe here. My name's Patrick, and you, what should I call you?"

"Why you take me here?" I pick up broken bottle, I jab him—

"Whoa, whoa, lass."

I jab bottle closer—"You tell me where's Joe? What did you do with Joe?"

He twists my hand, bottle crashes. "Now, we'll have none

of that, there is no Joe here. My name is Patrick." He pushes me towards chair. Where am I? Heaven hell heaven—

"You must be hungry."

He brings me a piece of bread and cup of water. I grab it and shove it in my mouth squinting at this blue-eyed man.

"Now, now, slow down, slow down, it will go down easier." He gives me another piece. My mama warned me of the blue-eyed devils. He takes a puff on his pipe, smoke rises above us, is he praying to the ancestors? "Now what do you call yourself?"

I eat the bread—should I run and find Joe? Maybe Papa will find me.

"So, no words?"

"Where's Joe! Where's Joe!" I get up, go outside on porch— "Papa! Joe! Papa, Joe! Where are you?" He holds me down—I fight him, I fight, I fight. My body goes limp. I stop. I can't move anymore.

"There, there." He leads me back to barrels and bottles room. He brings me more bread. He makes tea, singing as he makes it. I sit. I eat. I drink. I don't know where Joe is I don't know where I am I am lost. I miss my mama. I can feel her soft dark hand on my cheek. "Mama?" I reach out for her, she gets up to leave.

"Mama!" She vanishes. What world have I entered? Papa speaks to me.

Let me tell you how I met your mother. She came to me in a dream first—as a sick deer with big eyes. She showed me the plants that heal. I helped her dig them out and fed them to her. She got better and never left me.

Two black women came to my door, Aunt Julia and Mary. Mary was leaning on Aunt Julia barely able to stand. Mary had the same eyes as the deer in the dream, I recognized her, and she recognized me.

"They say you are a healer." Aunt Julia approached me. "They won't take blacks at the hospital. I'm Julia and this is my sister

Mary. She's got TB, I don't have much, this is what I have." *Julia gave me a small purse. I couldn't take my eyes off Mary.* "Wait," *I said, and I ran out the door into the forest. I ran to the woods in the dream. I offered the plants tobacco, thanked them first and dug them out. I ran as fast as I could back home and boiled the herbs for Mary to drink. Slowly your mama regained her strength, and her coughing stopped. She came to the forest with me, to offer tobacco to the plants. She helped pull up the roots. She stayed with me and learned the ways of the medicine.*

We had a wedding, and she was my wife. She helped people who came for medicine, some Indian, some black, we helped whoever came. And you little one was born, and then Joe. The sickness came back, this time it was too strong. I prayed for a dream and fasted in the forest waiting to find the medicine that would save Mary, my love. It rained, sharp, cold rain, the coldness too strong, it took your mama, it was time for her to go. It was her time.

His voice stops, I reach out my hands to catch him—gone. "Papa!" Father Sun rises—I run outside to catch it, to the edge of the river. Across the river is a great bear, he stands on his hind legs. "Papa!" I rush into the river my arms outstretched—he turns around and walks into the woods.

"Lass, you're going to catch a death out here!" Bird Man's voice startles me. The river is cold, I want my papa. "Come on, love, come here." He picks me up, carries me back to the house, gently places me on the bed and pulls the blanket over my shivering body.

Back to sleep. I don't know how long I sleep, a day? Birds are talking in the house. Walk into bottle and barrel room, there he is making bird calls out of his mouth, he stops.

"Well, there she is, awake now? There's a potato for you to eat for we've got a long journey." Empty bottles, full bottles with clear liquid cover the floor. "Come on, lass, get going." I sit down at table and eat. Bird Man makes his bird sounds as he rushes, filling bottles, screwing in wood corks on top. "We are taking a journey down the river, yes, we are going to sell these spirits." I finish potato. "Come here now and fill this bottle." He hands me bottle and shows me how to fill it. It smells sharp to my nose. I liked how it made me feel in the canoe, warm, light, like I was floating. I fill bottles and put cork on top, we put in a box. Many boxes. Many bottles. He starts bird calling again even dances some jerky motion, knees in air. I laugh, laugh so hard at this strange dancing Bird Man.

"So now I know you laugh, eh?" He stops his silly dance. "Come, let's load the canoe."

He wraps potatoes in sack, puts on his hat and we carry boxes to canoe. In canoe I am surrounded by boxes of spirit bottles. The river talks its familiar sound, this river I know. We follow it a long time. Sometimes I take the paddle, Bird Man sings and we eat potatoes. I start to recognize the land; this river Papa and the men would fish in—I'm going home? The strange Bird Man is taking me home?

"Well that's about it," he says. We pull canoe to the side of the bank, at a pier with ships. We hide the canoe. He gives me basket with bottles covered with a blanket. He slips bottles in his boots and walks funny, slow like an old man. We walk up bank to dirt street. Smell of fish, rotting fish, a factory, sardine factory, men and women swarm out of building. We stand in dirt street. Bird Man moves his feet nervously—men know him, they come and ask for a pint, give him money, he reaches into his boot and hands them a shiny bottle. More and more men come by, stop to talk with Bird Man, they laugh—give money, get bottle. They all talk like Bird Man, same bubble stream talk—all white men. Most of them hairy, they happy to see Bird Man, happy to get their bottle.

We run out of bottles and walk back to canoe to get more. Bird Man whistles. "Not a bad day, lass, not a bad day at all." He fills the basket and his boots, we walk back to our spot. A few men come to buy some bottles. A man in a blue suit with stick comes towards us—is he an agent? I freeze—Bird Man hands a man a bottle. Is the agent going to take me back to the school? He takes Bird Man's arm, men scatter.

"What are you selling here?" The man in blue suit carries a stick, like the stick that beat Papa down. Bird Man tries to slip bottle in his pocket. Blue suit man catches him, Bird Man raises bottle up. "Just an elixir, just an elixir, sir."

"Is that right?" Blue suit man is a big man, wide shoulders and a barrel stomach.

"Yes sir." Bird Man's hands tremble.

"Well, let me see." Blue suit man takes bottle, opens cork and sniffs. "This is no elixir."

"I can explain, sir"

"It is against the law to sell alcohol in Maine." Blue suit taps his stick.

"Yes sir, yes sir, let me explain."

Maybe I should run. Blue suit gets real close to Bird Man and whispers, "I tell you what, you give me three pints and I'll forget the whole thing."

"Sure, sure, officer, sure." Bird Man gives two more bottles to blue suit who slips them in his coat.

"Now git!" he shouts, walking away, swinging his stick.

"That was a close one." Bird Man smiles.

"Why didn't he take me?" I say.

"Take you? Why in the world would he want to take you?" Bird Man laughs. "Now come on, lass, let us get some dinner after all our hard work." Bird Man sings and every so often does some jerky steps. I catch his coattails and walk behind him, peeking out to make sure blue suit doesn't come after me.

We enter a loud dark bar, music playing, happy music, feet stomping, men and women clapping hands. Women painted faces, red lips like cranberries. They all know Bird Man, crowd around him, slap his back, smile, we sit at a booth. Bird Man brings out more bottles, he is the hero, the hero of the spirits.

A lady brings food: fish fried, cabbage, potatoes. I eat so much. Bird Man laughs with woman, tight dress showing her bosom. Woman takes Bird Man, they leave, I stay and eat.

"Here's a young one, a darkie," a man yells, red in the face, bottle in hand, swaying towards me. "How much for her? I bet she must be a virgin!" He leans over me; his breath smells sour. "I've never had a dark one like you yet, let me show you a ride tonight, show you how it's done, how much—how much?" He kisses me, my body freezes, his hand slides down my shirt, he squeezes my breast. "Ooooh, like that? How much, lass?"

I kick, howl, try to get out of his arms, music so loud, he won't let go—he picks me up, I try and get away—where is Bird Man? I scream again.

"Oh, I like that—a feisty one!"

He carries me to room it's dark. He pulls my shirt off, squeezing breasts. He hits me, I fall. He undoes his pants, voices outside the door, a man and woman tumble in.

"How's this room?" she says. The man squeezes her, she giggles.

"Alright, lass." It's Bird Man's voice. I'm on floor, man standing over me.

"What are you doing with her?" Bird Man moves closer.

"What? This darkie isn't worth nothing!"

"She's just a child, you louse!" Bird Man takes bottle in hand and smashes it on man's head. He falls like a tree and gets up like a bear, punching. Bird Man falls down—the woman screeches. I put my clothes back on and Bird Man gets up and slugs him. The man falls, I pick up a chair and smash it on man's back. He goes down. Bird Man picks up his hat and takes my hand. "Come now, lass, time to go." He doesn't let go of my hand, the woman with painted lips hugs Bird Man.

"What about us?"

He squeezes her behind. "Another time." We gather our things and walk out on street. Bird Man leads us back to the bank, to canoe, he is quiet, he makes no bird sounds.

The moon is out, stars are out. Bird Man covers me with a blanket and paddles up the river. I sleep, that night in the canoe, I dream a big owl comes to me, it's Joe, I know it's Joe, he hoots at me and flies away. Joe is talking from spirit land—I know Joe is dead. They caught him, tied him to a tree that's what they did, like they did to the other one, his lifeless body slumped over, we couldn't help him—

I have no one. Mama died, Papa died from agent's stick, Joe died, Bird Man all I have. We make many trips down river selling spirits. He caught me but I caught him. After that night at the bar, Bird Man hold my hand, more careful. Spirits—selling spirits, that's how we survived. I drank spirits. Spirits help me forget. Bird Man drank to stop sadness in his eyes. He was forgetting something too? Many years go by. I have babies—one die, one live, a girl, Deliah, she help with our spirit selling. We make our own, we survive, that's how we survive.

DELIAH

Eastport, Maine

RIVER SPIRITS

Papa was an Irish man, he used to sing to me—all kinds of songs—we lived by the river near Eastport. Mama and Papa had a moonshine business. We were poor, but we had food, potatoes, lots of them. We turned them into moonshine, and we ate them. Had a small garden in front of our two-room shack with wood plank floors. We stored the potatoes under a wood plank, it was the middle one that was easy to raise up. The river sang songs to me. Mama told me there were river spirits and if you stayed long enough—you could see them dancing on the water. I waited and waited for a spirit to appear—I think I saw one, I think I did.

I'd go with them to town to sell their moonshine. Mama always kept me hidden, she was afraid someone was going to snatch me—especially the white people. I was fair, I had my papa's auburn hair. He'd say: "That's the Irish in you, lass."

"Papa, what's Irish?" I'd respond, and he'd laugh, smoke his pipe and sing me a song from Kerry, where his people came from. Every night before I went to sleep, Papa would sing to me.

"Papa, sing me a song!"

"Okay, lass, what song should I sing . . ." Papa teased me.

"The rose song! The rose song!"

"Hmmmm, I wonder, where is that song from?"

"From Ireland, Papa, you know that!"

"Oh, yes, how does it go again?"

And so, I started it:

"Come over the hills, my bonny Irish lass,
Come over the hills to your darling."

And Papa continued with his deep voice:

"You choose the rose, love,
And I'll make the vow,
And I'll be your true love forever." His voice became mournful:
"It's not for the loss of my only sister Kate
It's not for the loss of my mother;
'Tis all for the loss of my bonny Irish lass,
That I'm leaving Ireland forever." And I'd chime in,
"Red is the rose that in yonder garden grows,
And fair is the lily of the valley
Clear is the water that flows from the Boyne,
But my love is fairer than any."

"Papa," I asked, "is this song true?"

His blue eyes watered. "Why yes, yes." He took out his pipe, put tobacco in it and lit it with a match.

"How did they lose each other?"

"Hmm?" He puffed his pipe.

"The mother got lost, the sister and the bonny lass. How did they get lost? Did they ever get found again?"

"No, dear, no, there was a famine."

"What is a famine?"

"It is when there is no more food, and we the Irish counted on potatoes to survive and one awful harvest, they turned black and rotten and people, well, they starved . . . to death. Babies, mothers, families. 'Twas awful, awful. I was born towards the end of it; it took my whole family. Fortunately, I had a good master, a decent master, and after my whole family perished, he took pity on me and got me a ticket to America. I was a young lad, I barely made it here, most died on the ship, a floating coffin . . . but God willing and with Saint Christopher's aid, I survived by the skin of my own teeth and learned the moonshine business. I was not going to starve again. No, we will never starve here, my dear, never." He took me in his arms and kissed my forehead. "Now off to bed, lass, off to bed." And I curled up in my cot dreaming of roses, and water spirits.

Sundays, Papa took me to church in Eastport. We'd row the canoe down the river, hide it in the bank and carefully climb out trying not to muddy our Sunday clothes. Mama wouldn't go; she'd pack a lunch pail for us and stand on the riverbank as we glided past her. Mama didn't like church, said it spread poison, said the poison was still in her. I liked it. I liked the smell of wood and incense, the grand organ and the cross. My papa took me because he said he didn't want me growing up "heathen." Every Sunday we went, that is, until he got sick.

It happened slowly. His skin turned yellow, his eyes sunken, body thin and frail. My mama called it the "drinking disease." She said many of her people died of it. I tried to stop his drinking, afraid he was dying, so I hid bottles behind a bush. One by one I carried them under my dress while my mama was cooking. I was going to make the bottles disappear so Papa wouldn't. A bottle slipped and smashed to the floor. Mama startled and raised a wooden spoon. Papa was snoozing in the rocking chair. Mama charged after me with the spoon in the air and I ran as fast as I could, dodging her—until Papa woke up. It was too late; she got me on the ground and beat me with the wooden spoon. Papa, as frail as he was, tried to get in between us but Mama wouldn't stop—

"Emma, Emma darling, put it down, put it down," Papa cried out. Mama backed away and dropped the spoon.

"She was stealing the bottles, our bottles, Patrick."

"There, there, Deliah, get up now and no more taking the bottles." He didn't know I was trying to save him, he didn't know.

* * *

It is Sunday—I pray that Papa will rise from his bed so we can glide down the river to church. His breathing rattles, his eyes a glint of blue—he is a shrunken version of what he used to be.

"Sing me a song, Deliah, sing me a song." His voice is raspy. So, I begin:

"Red is the rose that in yonder garden grows, and fair is the lily of the valley . . ." Maybe the singing is making him better, so I keep singing: "Clear is the water that flows from the Boyne, but my love is fairer than any." Papa starts writhing in his bed, I stop singing—

"The famine took them, all of them, can't you see them, lass? Skeletons all of them—what are they doing here? Oh—my mum, my mum." His frail arms stick out like thin branches. "Mum!" Mama rushes in with a wet cloth and places it on his forehead. I run out to the river to find a river spirit to help. The water rushes past me as silver fish flicker around my legs. No spirits are here yet; they will come. Jesus, God, Mary help us. I wait for hours until light wanes from the sky and Mama starts singing in the old language. I run into our shack and into the bedroom. Mama burns sweetgrass over Papa, smoke fills the room. I don't understand her singing. I don't know what she is saying. My father lies stiff on the bed, his eyes are closed. My feet are cold and dripping from the river. Papa is gone. I am seven years old.

Where is God? Where is Jesus? Where are the river spirits? I've never seen Mama cry and she wails as she digs a deep hole behind the house. I start to help, and I wail with her. We dress Papa in his Sunday clothes and carry him to the hole. We place him in sitting upright; his head flops forwards. I ask Mama why he is sitting, she says so he will be ready to go when it's time. I don't want to leave him there. We walk back to the house. Mama tells me to get his things. She gets his hat and a bottle of moonshine and I pick up his pipe and bible. We walk to the hole and Mama places the hat and bottle near Papa's sunken figure. I put his pipe next to him and take out his bible, then decide to hide it under my dress. This hole is where Papa lives now. Mama and I weep and wail as we cover him with dirt. Mama gives me some moonshine to calm me down that night.

FIRE

Mama says we are going to Brunswick to stay with her Aunt Julia. She's busy packing a lunch pail of dried salmon and potatoes. She points to a bag. "Pack it, we're leaving." I run to the corner where my cot is and place my bedding and my good dress in the bag. I get Papa's bible from underneath my cot and tuck it carefully in the bag. I help Mama lift the baskets into the canoe. She wraps a bag around her back; I carry my bag like a big girl. "Where are we going, Mama?"

"Brunswick, I told you Brunswick."

"Where is that?"

"Where Aunt Julia lives, we will find her."

"Why?"

"Because it is not good to live with the dead."

Yes, I want to leave too. I try to picture Brunswick in my mind. Mama walks to the still and rolls a barrel to the side of the house. Now it seems so lonely, vacant. She empties the barrel, strikes a match and drops it. The side of the house shoots up in flames. She says something in the old language, then steps away from the house.

"Why, Mama?" I ask.

"Now Patrick can see the river."

I help her pull the canoe out to the shore, and we climb in, careful not to tip over. We drift down the river in silence as flames consume our house, lighting the night sky.

We paddle underneath a wharf in Eastport. Long wooden planks hold up a sardine factory above us. The smell of rotting fish sickens me. Mama hides the canoe and we unload our bags. We walk underneath tall planks along the side of the factory and up a bank. Mama carries the basket with the bottles and we step onto the dirt street. Factory workers scurry past us, some recognize Mama and ask for a bottle. A white man with a brown cap and beard nods at her. Mama lifts the white cloth covering the bottles and quickly slips him a bottle. He hands her a coin, hides the bottle in his sleeve and hurries off. We stay on that street until all the bottles are gone. Most of the time I hide my face in Mama's skirt like she told me to do. We walk back to the canoe and Mama pushes it into the water. The river takes it under the starry sky. Mama bends down scraping wet dirt into her hands, and she pulls me to her, rubbing the dirt on my face. "Still," she commands and I don't squirm because I know blows will come if I do.

"Why, Mama?"

"You need to be darker." She wipes her hands on her skirt, and I follow behind her as we climb the bank to the factory and onto the street. Children run past us in ragged clothes and bare feet, a loud bell rings and people rush out of the factory. Bodies bump into us. I cling to Mama's skirt as hard as I can all the way to the railroad station.

At the station Mama speaks to a man behind a window and says, "Two, Brunswick." He glances over to me and I hide my face.

"Next train is in two hours." Mama gives him money and gets the tickets. We head outside and sit on a bench facing the tracks.

The screeching sound of the train startles me. I lift my head and in front of me is the giant metal creature. It's the first time I've seen a train. We climb aboard and find our seats. I take the window seat and say goodbye to the river as the train chugs away.

"Brunswick!" the conductor yells. Mama shakes me awake, and we gather our bags and head down the aisle. The conductor helps me off the train. He has dark skin like the dirt Mama rubbed on my face. We walk through the depot station and sit on the steps. Mama takes a piece of dried salmon from the lunch pail and hands me a piece. In front of the depot, an Indian family sells baskets. We approach them and Mama offers them dried salmon. They talk in the old language I don't understand. I miss Papa.

We say our goodbyes to the family and Mama hurries me along past the train station and onto the crowded street. Lines of cars are parked on the side of the huge dirt road. Ladies dressed in fancy skirts and huge hats with satin bows stroll in pairs stopping at storefronts. We pass a market with wooden crates of overflowing oranges and apples. I pull Mama's skirt. "I'm hungry," I say. We rest on a bench and she gives me the last bit of dried salmon.

"Sleep," Mama commands. Images of Papa in the hole, the house burning in flames, flood my head. I lay my head in Mama's lap, willing myself to hear Papa singing.

Sun peeks through the clouds. People are milling about on the street. Mama takes ahold of me and rubs more dirt on my face. My tummy rumbles; I'm hungry. Mama sits us down right in the middle of people passing, places the empty lunch pail in front of us and pulls me in her lap. We wait for people to drop coins in our pail. Some people ignore us; others rush past us shaking their heads in scorn. Someone spits at us; a few people drop coins in our pail.

Mama counts the coins and we gather our belongings and walk to a market. Mama buys salami and bread, we sit on a bench and eat. We walk, we walk so long, past the busy streets, farmhouses, fields; we walk until sundown. We approach a small house with a water pump in the front yard. Mama points to the house. "Aunt Julia." As we come closer, a group of dark children run to greet us. They surround me, asking questions.

"Who are you?"

"Are you Indian?"

"Where you from?"

Except one sullen boy with big eyes is quiet. Mama steps up to the front porch and knocks on the door. A dark woman with a face as round as the moon opens it.

"Emma?" She says wiping her hands on her apron.

"Auntie." Mama's eyes water, she pulls me in front of her. "This is Deliah."

Aunt Julia pats my head. "Oh that hair chile and those smart eyes! Hmmm, you all need to get cleaned up, you must been walking for hours. We don't have a lot of space but y'all are welcome, Deliah and Emma. Boys! Get some water for the tub." The boys scamper out, the sullen one lags behind. He glances at me before he rushes out the door. The tub is set in the back of the room separated by a curtain. Mama scrubs me in the tub as I listen to Aunt Julia sing. Mama makes a pallet for me to sleep on with a blanket and old towel. I fall asleep to the sound of Aunt Julia's deep voice.

The morning light makes me squint. Mama is already moving about the kitchen with Aunt Julia. Three boys crowd around me. I pull the blanket over my head. One pokes me. "Is she awake?"

"Does she talk?" another voice asks. I throw the blanket off and shout for my mama, running to the folds of her skirt. "I guess she can talk." They laugh and run outdoors. Mama hands me a biscuit and motions me to sit down at the table. Aunt Julia reassures me.

"Now Deliah, those children don't mean a thing. Just eat your biscuit and join them outside, they'll show you around." I finish my biscuit, climb off the chair, and put on my dress and shoes, curious to find out what they are doing outside. I've never been around other children before, except at church with Papa. They all sat still like me—afraid of moving too much to cause alarm to the adults around them. These boys have dark skin, darker than the dirt Mama rubbed on my face, dark like Aunt Julia's. When Aunt Julia smiled, her white teeth shone, unlike

Mama who didn't smile much at all.

Outside, the boys chase each other except for the quiet boy who digs the dirt with his toe and every so often glances sheepishly at me. I stand close to him as the others play, kicking up dirt as they race past us. The boy is a head taller than me; his eyebrows knit together like he's trying to solve a mystery.

"Where did you come from?"

"The river," I say.

"How'd you get here?"

"A train." I want to run with the other children but I don't know what they're playing.

"What's your name?"

"Deliah, what's yours?"

"Henry. Are you Indian?"

"I'm Irish."

"You're Indian, that's what they say."

One of the boys tags me, "You're it!" They all laugh and scamper away from me.

"Go on," Henry says. "Go on and catch someone, don't you know how to play tag?"

I chase the boys—even sullen-eyes Henry plays. I catch the smallest one, he cries, so I go after another boy. They run in circles around me until I'm tired. Aunt Julia shouts from the door, "Come on, children, time to do your chores—enough of that playing." I follow the boys, mimicking them as they pull weeds in the garden, feed the chickens, fetch water from the pump, until Mama calls me in and I help peel potatoes in the kitchen.

After chores, we eat lunch and get to play again. The boys can't wait and they burst out the door. I follow behind them. Henry asks me, "Where's your father?"

I stop in my tracks. The afternoon air is warm with a slight breeze. "At the river," I say. My poor papa sits in a hole so far away from me. I push the thought away. "Where's yours?"

"Dead." He picks up a stone and throws it as far as he can.

"But your mama is here."

"She ain't my mama, my mama in Boston."

"Where's that?"

"That's a big city where she works for white people." He scampers off, joining the others in a game of hide and seek.

At dinner a tall dark man enters, takes off his hat, wipes his brow with a kerchief and sits down at the head of the table. Aunt Julia embraces him and fetches him a cool drink of water.

"How were the horses today, Isaiah?"

"As they always are, Julia. Mucked plenty of stalls and rode plenty of horses. I see we got company." He nods at me and Mama.

"Yes, yes, this is Emma and her daughter Deliah."

Mama says nothing and wipes her hands on her apron. She places a bowl of stew and corn bread in front of him.

"Isn't it enough we have the grandkids and took in Henry?" Isaiah stabs at the stew and swallows a big spoonful.

"Wasn't your nephew's fault he died on the street without no doctor's care." Aunt Julia shakes her head. "I'm not turning family away. Emma is family."

"Everyone is family to you." Isaiah takes a swig of water.

"That's right, honey, and the good Lord would want it that way." Aunt Julia flashes her smile at him. He finishes his meal, gets up slowly and smokes his pipe on the porch.

After dinner, Aunt Julia gathers us all in front of the fire for story time. She sits in the grand rocking chair and we all sit on the floor staring at her with obedient eyes. Mama is busy cleaning up the supper dishes.

"Now children, I am an old woman, but I used to be youngins like y'all. I come from a big family, the Freemans, yes, free mans cause we born free. My sister Mary, Emma's mother, was born free too, but she die of coughing disease. Not everyone was born free back then; no, they slaves, born slaves just like my great-grandpa Paul Freeman. You all remember his name cause that is why you here in Maine. He was a big man, born a slave in Massachusetts, that's where your mama is, Henry, working for them white folks. But she free—he wasn't free. He had a family—they's wasn't free neither. Then there was this war, you see, white folks fighting each other, the white folks that live here in America wanted their freedom. Ain't that something? White folks wasn't free from other white folks, but black folks not free from white folks. Anyhow, white folks in America wanted freedom from them other British white folks, so there was a war. And my great-grandpa Paul, he was smart. He saw an opportunity to get free, and he fought in that white people's war and the white Americans won, they got their freedom, so Great-grandpa Paul, you know what he'd done?" All of our eyes are open wide and you can't hear a sound but the fire crackling. "He done got his freedom from fighting in that white people's war, and he took his family to Brunswick and that's how I came and that's how you all came. So children, you are somebody, you free, you come from Freeman. Now wash up and get to bed." Everyone gets up except Henry, he sits in front of the rocking chair with his brows knit together.

"Aunt Julia?"

"Yes, Henry."

"What about Granduncle Isaiah, he a Freeman?"

"Your granduncle, no, but he a fighter too."

"How?"

"I met your granduncle Isaiah when my brother Augustus came back from the war that freed the slaves. He brought Isaiah home with him. Isaiah fought alongside Augustus with the colored soldiers so he fought for his freedom too, yes he did. Augustus lost an arm, but Isaiah you see intact. My family took him in. That's what we did, took people in, made them our own. Now we together, I loved him first time I seen him."

"What stories you telling, Julia?" Isaiah puts his hands on her shoulders.

"I'm telling him you is a fighter." Julia rocks in her chair.

"Come here, boy," Isaiah orders Henry. Henry quickly gets up and stands in front of Isaiah. "Yes, I am, fought for everything I got, still fighting, son. Don't you ever give up. You come from warriors."

"Yes sir, I won't forget."

Isaiah pats Henry's head. "Now go on to bed now with the others."

Henry leaves carrying himself a little higher with his chest puffed up and pride in his eyes. He finds a spot on the bed with the other boys and goes to sleep.

We stayed at Aunt Julia's until the Indian man came to visit. Granduncle Isaiah brought him: his name was Charles. He ate with us and Mama served him. He spoke the old language with Mama and she spoke back.

The rooster crows. Mama shakes my legs and tells me to pack my bag. I throw my blanket off; the floor is cold underneath my bare feet. I slide my cotton dress over my head and put on my coat. I pack my one nice dress, blanket and Papa's bible in my bag. I wait for Mama on the porch. Henry, sullen as usual, strolls over to me.

"Where you going?"

"Don't know."

"Well, ain't you leaving?"

"Maybe I am. Maybe I'm going back home," I say, squeezing the bag against my chest.

Quick as a flash Henry kisses my cheek. "I'm gonna marry you one day." And he runs off into the yard. I quickly wipe the wet mark his lips imprinted on my cheek. We left that day, the Indian man Charles came with a horse and a cart. Mama picked me up and placed me in the cart and climbed in next to me. We waved goodbye to Aunt Julia who flashed her brilliant smile, and the boys ran alongside the cart as far as they could. Henry stayed behind leaning against the front door; those big eyes I would see again, yes, I would.

BEAR SPIRIT

I called him Papa Charles. We had a small place, close to the town. We lived near lots of other Indian families. People came to Papa Charles and asked him for help. They brought him food and other gifts and Papa Charles would light sage and talk in the old language. It was mysterious. I never knew what they were saying though I felt something deep. Mama grew potatoes and began making moonshine—I helped. Papa Charles hunted deer and fished, still at times we went hungry. I liked going down to the bay where Papa Charles fished in his canoe. Sometimes he'd catch a seal, or fish using nets. Every day the water called me and I'd say a prayer for my papa. Once a great blue heron swooped above me and I was sure it was Papa sending me a good luck message.

Beatrice was born. I was a big girl, eight years old. I cared for her even though Mama didn't ask me to. I sang her to sleep like Papa did for me. My baby Beah, that's what I called her. As she started to walk, she'd follow me around as I pulled weeds, fetched water, and helped Mama with the still. Mama kept having babies, one after the other. By the time Beah was eight there was Mary, seven, Eleanor, six, and Samuel Joe, four. Samuel Joe was Mama's favorite, she made sure I kept an eye on him. Mama beat all of us except him, wouldn't lay a hand on him. Papa Charles never hit us, but Mama, when she was in one of her moods, we would clear out of her way.

I'd walk with Mama to town and we'd sell moonshine to the speakeasies. I loved the music; I'd come home humming songs. I was excited to enter the world of music and pretty women. I wanted to be one of those women; I studied them and practiced their faces at home.

* * *

Everything changed the day the agents came. Papa Charles had gone fishing. I was helping Mama peel potatoes to boil. They barged in without knocking, walking in like they owned the place, like they owned us—

Samuel Joe hid in Mama's skirts. Beah, Mary, and Eleanor ran to me. The agent's black boots clicked as he walked. "We got a full house here . . . four children school age." His partner made notes in a small book. The agent with the black boots pointed his stick at me. "How old are you?"

Mama's face froze with rage. "You can't come here!" She charged after him and he held her wrists effortlessly. Mama kicked him. "Get out! Get out of here!"

"Ma'am, if you continue like this we will have to arrest you. This is a Federal Ordinance, all Indian children must be sent to residential school, which is a step up from this place."

One by one the children started weeping, a chorus of sorrow. Mary, Eleanor and Beah ran to me and clutched onto my legs, arms and side, bawling as they held on. My mama thrashed about wailing, trying to shake off the agent—the other agent grabbed Mary and Eleanor, and picked them up as their limbs flailed in the air. The black boot agent threw Mama to the ground and snatched Beah and she held onto me so hard her nails ripped my sides as he pulled her off. He checked me over. "You're too old to go to school." He carried Beah away, following behind his partner. I went after them but it was too late. They put the children in a bus just like the ones in town.

I ran back to help Mama. The black boot agent seized Samuel Joe and Mama shrieked. Black boots threw Mama back, she fell, got back up, charged after him. He raised his stick and cracked it on her head, she crumpled. The agent left with Samuel Joe in his arms. "Damn Indians!" Mama was unconscious lying on the floor. I gave one last attempt to rescue

Samuel Joe, his little arms grappled for me as the other agent snatched him, forcing him onto the bus. The door shut, black boots held me back. "This is better for them, they're going to school." Black boots clasped his huge arms around me. "Come on, you can show me a good time." His beard bristled against my face, his breath smelled nasty. I shoved his face away and he smacked me on the mouth and knocked me to the ground. Blood dribbled down the side of my lip. "I don't have time for this," he grunted and stepped onto the bus. The blood tasted sharp in my mouth. The bus rolled down the dirt road and the whimpers of children faded.

I don't remember what happened after that, how I got off the ground or where I found Mama in the house. I couldn't forget Beah and the others. I couldn't forget their howling from the tin can bus. After that day, we lived in unbearable silence. Papa Charles came home to an empty nest. Moonshine helped: we made it, we sold it, we drank it. Papa Charles went fishing one day and never came back. Did the silence get to him? The thick air of pain? Our neighbor said Papa Charles walked into the bay until the water covered his head and a wave crashed over him and out came a porpoise. He said Papa Charles used his medicine to turn into a porpoise and he was watching over us from the bay, that he would protect us from there. I walked to the bay one time and a porpoise leaped out of the water. Maybe it was him, maybe it was Papa Charles.

The speakeasy is my heaven. Smoke-filled rooms ringing with laughter and music give me hope. Mama and I sell our moonshine there—it's always a party. I especially adore the singer, Eva. I want to be Eva, tall, dark and glamorous, commanding the stage with a drink in her hand, dressed in a beautiful gown and red lipstick. I sing along with her, quietly mouthing the words. Mama shushes me. I am mesmerized by the stage, by Eva.

Eva sings "You Can't Keep a Good Man Down," swaying to

the beat of the piano, punctuating the notes with her hips. She catches me mouthing the words, pulls me onstage. "Go on, girl, you can sing, I know you want to." I catch up with the piano and belt out the words in the right place. The crowd cheers, I finish the song, the piano punches to the end, abrupt applause and whistles fill the air. Eva pouts her lips and wags her finger at me. "You're gonna take my job, honey." She pats me on the head, downs her drink and steps off the stage. Mama is stunned, men buy me drinks. "You sure are pretty!" one hollers. "Sing another one!" another man calls out. Mama yanks me off the stage and out the door. She beat me when we got home.

"You won't be a harlot!" she yelled as the stick came down on me, but I didn't stop singing—my voice—that's all I had.

* * *

The children were gone a year; it took us that long to save money for the train tickets to get them. That is Mama's plan—to go to the school and get back her children. I am seventeen almost a grown woman. At the train station in Brunswick the memory of my first train ride hit me: Mama smearing dirt into my face so I would look like her child, so they wouldn't take me away. Now I understand. Mama sits in silence staring out the window the whole ride. I am jittery, humming songs running through my head. It takes a day to get there. We step off the train and walk down a winding dirt road. A large brick building sits menacingly on a hill. Mama lights sage before we continue and speaks the old language, sending wafts of smoke around us. I ask Mama, "What if they take me?"

"The bear spirit is with us, I have asked her to come." She snuffs out the sage on the ground. I steady myself and follow behind Mama's sure footsteps to the entrance of the school. Mama rings the doorbell. It is eerily quiet. A white nun in a habit opens the door slightly. "My children, I am here to get my children," Mama says fiercely.

"It is not visiting hours. It is dinner time." She tries to shut the door, Mama barges in.

"My children, I am here to get them." Mama glares at her, almost through her.

The nun steps back, flustered. "Well, what are their names and ages?" She takes a small pad of paper and pen from her pocket.

"Beah, nine, Samuel Joe, five, Mary, eight, and Eleanor, seven."

"Yes, well, I'll see what I can do." Her face is beet red in her white habit. Mama sits in a cushioned chair, her eyes fixated on the door. We wait. It is eerily quiet in the waiting room, no children's voices, nothing. The door opens and the nun enters with a scrawny girl. It's Beah, she is much skinnier and has dark circles under her eyes. Beah doesn't run to me or Mama, she waits for a prompt from the nun like a trained animal. The nun nods her head and Beah walks to us. We embrace her small body. Beah's arms hang limp at her sides and her face is vacant. Mama pulls away. "The others? Samuel Joe?" She juts her chin out ready to charge. Two more nuns appear in fancy habits. "The others—where are my other children?" Mama clenches her fists; her mouth hardens into a line.

"Yes, well, the others were sickly . . ." the first nun says. She steps back and bows her head. The tallest nun, who wears a black and white habit, clasps her hands in front of her. "I regret to inform you that your other children became ill and died of consumption. They are with the Lord now." Mama's breath fills her chest, like she will explode. The black and white habit nuns leave, the flushed nun in the white habit remains, immobilized by Mama's eyes. Mama turns towards Beah, takes her skinny arm and heads for the door.

"Where are you going?" the flushed nun asks.

"Three are dead, she will live," Mama says. She doesn't wait for a response and opens the door. The nun weeps with her face in her hands as we shut the door.

* * *

Beah changed. She follows me around with quiet cat footsteps and hardly ever talks. Doesn't care to learn the songs I pick up at the speakeasy, she is a ghost version of her former self. Silence stretches around the three of us. One night, Mama's wails shatter the silence. "Not Joe, not Joe, why wasn't it me? Why wasn't it me? Samuel my baby, my babies, where are my babies!" She's drunk, pounds the table with a stick over and over. She swings at us, fast and hard. I run, trying to dodge her stick. Beah stands motionless with her arms to her sides, not even trying to block the hits. I take the blows for her. Mama yells, "You should have been the one to die not him, you should have died not him!" I lie over Beah's whimpering body trying to pull us both away from the beating, until Mama just stops, drops the stick and walks outside. I put Beah to sleep and drink moonshine to numb the pain. I hum songs from the speakeasy and I can't wait till it's time to go and sell our bottles.

I wear my new dress, careful not to step in mud along the dirt road to town. I wonder if Eva will be there, will she invite me onstage again? Mama smirks at me as if she is reading my thoughts. Chickadees flit from branch to branch, chirping a hopeful tune. Beah trails behind us with her head down. Maybe the music will bring her back to life.

In the speakeasy, ragtime bangs on the piano, the place is hopping. Eva sits on the edge of the stage surrounded by admirers, laughing and smoking a cigarette. Mama finds a place at the bar with Beah close to her. I step to the beat of the rag, moving to the piano player as his black fingers speed up and down the keys. Eva shouts, "Hey, it's the little singer!" Her admirers turn to me. "Why don't you show us what you got?" They carry me to the stage. I start singing "Dinah," the piano follows. I move the way Eva moves, shaking hips and shoulders, the crowd roars. Mama heads for the door with Beah behind her. I don't stop.

I sing louder, I sing so loud I force Mama out and away from me. I sing the last note as long as I can. The applause is so loud it drowns out the piano. He plucks the last notes out and people are hooting and hollering. The piano player takes my hand and leads me off the stage. He gives me a drink. "Good job little singer, drinks on me." I take a sip; it's sweet not bitter like moonshine.

People start shouting, "Chug! Chug! Chug!" So, I chug it down and slam the empty glass on a table. The crowd goes wild. A man hands me another drink, I drink that one too. Eva takes me under her arm. "You know, darling, there's one more thing for you to do." I smile, dizzy from all the drinks. She leads me upstairs and opens a door to a bedroom. "Don't you want to be a singer?" Eva smooths the bedspread out. A man enters, takes off his hat and Eva leaves. I don't get home until morning.

Mama and Beah goggle at me—"What are you looking at?" I snarl and flop down on my cot willing my headache to go away. They don't have any right judging me, I'm gonna get out of this place. I'm gonna be a famous singer. I keep performing at the speakeasy and word gets out I can sing, other clubs want me. That's how we met again, at a speakeasy. His eyes followed me the whole night—who could forget them?

After my set at the bar, me and the boys are drinking and having a grand old time. I didn't know who he was, this distinguished, dark and handsome man. His presence was stoic and regal, as though he were somehow set above all the rest of us. Hmmm I'd like to lay my head down on that sturdy chest of his. I catch his glance then flirt with the boys in the band. For a moment, our eyes lock, my body quivers a bit. Who is this man? He slides off his chair, with a drink in one hand and cigarette in the other.

"I believe I have met you before." His voice is deep and commanding.

"No, I believe we haven't." I turn away.

"Aunt Julia's place." He stands unmovable.

"Aunt Julia? What do you know about Aunt Julia?" I'm ready to give him a piece of my mind. His eyes, they are familiar.

"Deliah." He says my name like he is saying the most precious thing ever.

"You are . . . you are . . ." My mind races back to a group of boys chasing me in a yard full of chickens, and one boy steals a kiss from me.

"Henry. I am Henry." He puts his cigarette out on the bar ashtray.

"Oh, yes, Henry! I remember—old sullen eyes!"

"Sullen?" He flashes a smile.

"Yes, sullen, if there ever was a more mopey boy!" I laugh.

"I'm not moping now." He sits down on a bar stool next to me.

"Why, I believe you aren't. Pleased to meet you again, Henry." I offer my hand, he takes it and caresses it.

"Yes, Deliah, the pleasure is mine."

I slide my hand out of his grasp and take a sip of my drink. "Life sure is funny, one minute you're a child running barefoot in a yard full of chickens and then abracadabra, you're surrounded by a bar full of men. Hah!" The boys in the band laugh. Henry's jaw tenses, he's not laughing.

"Hey, Dee," the piano player chimes in, "what do you prefer, the chicken or the men?"

"You know how much I like chicken, but you know I like men a hell of a lot more!" I clink glasses with all the boys, finish my drink.

Henry interjects. "Let me buy you a drink."

"Sure, Henry, sure, I'll have what you're having."

He motions to the bartender and whispers in my ear, "You sure are fine, real fine." His hand is on my thigh.

I try not to show the tingling shooting through my body. The bartender places a scotch on the rocks in front of me. I take slow sips, keeping my eyes on Henry. "Don't get too fresh now."

His hand doesn't leave. "I've found you now and I'm not letting go."

"Oh really?" I challenge him.

"Yes, Deliah, really."

HENRY

Old Orchard Beach, Maine
1933

STEAM

She sings like a bird. She steps off the stage, red lips, light skin, auburn hair and those legs—a showstopper. The audience claps and cheers for her. A man in a top hat stops her, she smiles—who she talking to? Holding her drink I walk over to her, the man hands her a card, she's glowing. Who is that man? He heads towards the stage. I stand in front of Deliah and hand her the drink. Placing my hand on her back, I guide her to our table.

"Baby, that was real nice." She carefully puts the card in her purse. She takes a sip of her drink. "Who was that man?" I ask.

"Why do you want to know?" She smiles, takes a cigarette out of her purse, leans towards me. I light it. She tilts her head, exhaling smoke to the side.

I place my hand on hers. "Because I want to know."

She cocks her head to the side. "Jealous?"

"Maybe, baby."

She strokes my hand. "Would you believe if I told you that was the great Duke Ellington?" She takes a swig of her drink.

"He's here tonight, isn't he?"

"Darling—he asked me if I wanted to sing with him! Can you believe it?"

My stomach churns. "Why you want to go do that for?"

"Sing on tour? Duke Ellington? This could be my only break!"

"You don't have any business singing with the Duke or anyone else."

"I don't see a ring on my finger, Henry." She flicks her cigarette ashes in the ashtray—I'm sitting cool, this woman, how dare she? My whole body yearns for her—I want to possess her—I grasp her hands, pull her to me.

"You're mine." I kiss her, she kisses me back, takes my hand and we go to the dance floor and Duke and his band tear up the night for us. It felt like it was only for us, my Deliah, shining, glowing star. I know I have to work a little harder to get her.

She's limp in my arms, staggering to my car. I open the door and help her in. We are lit. The smell of her perfume imbues the air.

"Henry, Henry, how about one more drink?"

"No, no, Deliah, that's it. I'm taking you home."

"Home, home, I don't want to go home, I want to sing. I want to sing with the great Duke!" She weaves into me as I start the car.

"I need to take you home."

"See . . ." She shows me a card. "Rose Cummings Summer Hotel, that's where he is, go on now, Henry, drive me there. Drive me."

My stomach tightens, that same knot. "I'm driving you home, Deliah, like I told your mother."

"You're just trying to get on her good side. Ha!" She takes out a cigarette.

"Maybe I am, Deliah, maybe I am." We pull up to her place, a modest house, chipped paint, gray, dim—

"Well, Henry, well, you got me home." She flicks her cigarette out the window.

"I'm crazy about you, Deliah, you're my woman. I'm going to take care of you. I've got work, a car, it's only up for us, baby, the sky is the limit!"

"Henry, stop that crazy talk, we're in the middle of a

depression—haven't you heard?" She laughs, laughs at me. I take her in my arms, she doesn't resist. I kiss her. I could crush her small frame underneath me.

"Oh Deliah, Deliah." I run my hands up her dress, those legs, those thighs. She stops my hands.

"Henry, I said I want another drink."

"You've had too much already, Deliah."

"Well, I don't want to go in yet, I just don't." She presses her lips together in a pout, opens the door and gets out of the car.

"Where you going?"

"Well, if you won't drive me to the Summer Hotel, I'm walking. I am getting a drink and I'm going to sing with Ellington." Her heels sink into the mud, she almost falls over. Catches herself. "Goddamn these shoes!" She takes them off and heads on down the street.

"Deliah! Deliah!" I shout, and she keeps right on walking down the middle of the street. This woman, this woman, what is she doing to me?

"Now Deliah, Deliah, listen to me." I hold her shoulders and stand in front of her. "You're my woman, I'm going to take care of you—we're getting married, Deliah, I don't want to hear any more about this singing. I'll take you away from this place, we'll have our own place. Darling, darling Deliah." She puts her arms around my neck, her body sways from side to side, I steady her.

"You love me, Henry?"

I caress her face, the moon above our witness.

She sinks into my arms, and we stay that way in the middle of the street. I know I have caught her.

PORTLAND, MAINE
1934

I was making money when most people were starving. We were doing okay, got an apartment in Munjoy Hill, the only section of Portland they allow blacks. People needed their cars fixed. Sometimes they had no money and paid me in food, fried chicken, potatoes, I took it all. We were getting along. I knew this was a stepping stone for me. I knew I could do more. It's my birthday, I'm twenty-six. There's no snow yet although the air is frigid, the cold sea breeze gets inside your bones. I park the car on the street and head up to our apartment. My hands and clothes are covered with grease from working on cars all day. Least I'm working, yes—Lord, least I'm working. I open the door, it smells like smoke, Deliah is in the kitchen fanning the smoke with a towel.

She holds up a burnt mound of something. She begins to cry. "I'm sorry, honey, I was doing my best, I wanted your birthday to be special, and now . . . oh this smoke!" We both furiously fan the air. We start laughing, I throw my towel down and bring her to me. Smells of burnt sugar and grease waft in the air.

"Now let me get washed up, and meanwhile you put on that dress I like to see you in." I pat her bottom and head towards the washroom.

She dries her tears with her apron and walks to the bedroom to change.

Twenty-six years, twenty-six, my own father made it to thirty-three. I hardly remember him—my mother said she tried to bring him to the hospital, but they wouldn't take colored folk. And he died. He died an excruciating death—appendicitis.

My father shrieked on the ground, clutching his side. "Come on, James, you can make it." He leaned on my mother and I held onto the folds of her skirt. We walked, my father wincing in pain. Finally, we got to the hospital. Weary-eyed people sat in the waiting room. A white man in a straw hat, a pipe in his mouth, sneered at us as we hobbled inside. My mother led us to the front of the room and knocked on a door with a window. The window slid open. A woman in a white cap and thin pursed lips scowled. "We do not serve colored people here." She slammed the window.

My mother banged on the door. "Please, please, ma'am, he's not well, my husband, please where can I go? Please!" The door slid open. "Next," the woman commanded. My father hunched over my mother and fell to the floor. A white woman carrying her baby stepped in front of us.

"Come on James, get up, get up!" Mama pleaded. He staggered to his feet and we dragged him towards the door.

The man with the straw hat and pipe spat at us, "Niggers!" I raised my fist ready to slug him, my mother caught my arm and hauled us out of the hospital onto the street. My father collapsed on the ground. I think I remember him screaming, I think I do . . .

Hot water feels good wiping away all that grease. When I step out of the shower, Deliah is shining in her dress, putting on lipstick.

"Well, you've steamed it up in here, haven't you?" She wipes off the mirror, she's stunning. My Deliah. "Where are we going, Henry?"

"That joint on Main Street."

"Alright."

I get dressed, and we walk to the club. People in the neighborhood shout at us as we pass by. "Looking sharp!"

"Where you off to?"

"Lucky man!"

Deliah has her arm in mine, we strut like fine peacocks down the street. In the club, we find a table, order drinks as the band sets up. Deliah announces, "It's my man's birthday!" Folks come over, slap me on the back, buy me drinks. The band starts a jitterbug. I take Deliah's hand and we are swinging, baby, swinging woooh! I feel the pulse, the beat, Deliah spins for me, we hop in sync to the bass, the trumpet blares, the piano boogies and we are on fire.

1937

She took care of me most of the time. Margaret was born and she was real busy. I was building my knowledge and experience fixing cars, troubleshooting problems, building a reputation: "That Henry, he can fix your car," people said. This restlessness overcame me, then Deliah had twins. I was out most of the time because when I came home, she was sour to me.

"Where have you been, Henry?" she snarls at me the minute I walk in the door, a drink in her hand, hair disheveled. She loses her balance and falls into my chest. I can smell the booze. She's wearing the same clothes she woke up in, a blue faded house-dress with stains on the front. So homely, not like she used to dress, no, she used to light up a room. She doesn't smell like a woman, she smells like a damn drunk.

"I've been working."

"This late?"

"I've got new clients." I hang up my coat and hat. Little Margaret wobbles over. "What's for dinner?" I almost trip on a wooden toy on the floor. The place is a mess: clothes and toys are scattered everywhere. An empty bottle of gin and dirty dishes cover the coffee table. I kick the wooden toy out of my way. Damn I'm hungry.

"I left you a plate in the oven." The twins start fussing. She finishes her drink and picks up one of the boys. I eat and little Margaret sits on my lap, every now and then she takes a bite. Deliah comes back with Lloyd in her arms. Lloyd extends his stubby arms.

"Papa," he says with longing brown eyes.

"Hello, little man." I pat his head and finish eating. Margaret slides off my lap. Hank crawls into the kitchen, bawling. Deliah puts Lloyd down and picks up Hank.

"Now what do you want Hank?" she says, slurring her

speech. Lloyd crawls over to me and pulls on my leg, he starts bawling. My stomach tenses. I gently remove Lloyd's hands from my leg and get up.

"I've got to go." I head for the door.

"You just got here."

"You take care of my babies. I'll be back." I put my hat and coat on and fly out the door. I don't know where I'm heading but I'm out. I can't breathe in that apartment with all the children fussing all at once. Deliah pecks at me, nothing soft or nice, just peck, peck, peck, like a barn hen. I take a drive and end up at a bar. I walk into a fog of cigarette smoke, light chatter, and a mournful tune playing. I sit at the bar and order a drink. A woman in a black stylish hat with a green plumed feather tilted to the side sits at a table across the room. I nod my head, she nods back. I tell the bartender, "Give her a drink, on me."

"Sure." He places the drink on her table, her hat tips up as she asks the bartender something, he gestures to me. Her body freezes a moment. She picks up her purse and walks over to me.

"I thought that was you, Henry." I do a double take, it's dark in here. It's Beah. She's a grown woman now. Last time I saw her she was still playing with dolls.

"I didn't recognize you with that hat."

She smiles, full red lips, thick black hair, curves in all the right places. "Henry, what are you doing here?"

"Just getting some air."

She sips her drink, crosses her legs, teasing me with her sheer stockings with black lines running down the back.

"You're looking good." I smile.

"How are the babies?"

"Oh they're good, good . . ." I swirl my drink around. She nods, takes a cigarette out. I give her a light, she tilts back her head and exposes her smooth neck. Her large brown eyes reveal nothing, her lips, a faint smile? With no trace of her sister's frantic, birdlike movements Beah sits like a majestic cat, waiting—

I squeeze her thigh, and she opens her mouth slightly—I pull her to me.

"Come, Beah, come with me." She drops her arms to her sides, puts her cigarette out and we walk to my car. I drive to a secluded street and boy, do we steam up the car that night.

"You smell like a tramp!" Deliah hollers at me as I walk through the door.

"You're crazy, woman." I point to her. "And you've been drinking again." I mutter to myself, "There's no point in trying to change this woman."

"So have you."

"Not as much as you."

"I can't take this anymore, Henry, why, why do you leave me?"

"Clean up, Deliah, you're a mess." She drops to the ground weeping. "You're a messy drunk." I step over her.

"And you're a mean one, Henry, a mean one." I sleep on the couch that night.

The morning sun is too bright. I have a whopping headache, man, am I hung over. Margaret tugs at my sleeve. Can't this woman feed her children? I pick Margaret up and sit her at the kitchen table. The door to our bedroom is wide open. Deliah is sprawled across the bed, I tap her back.

"Margaret is hungry. I've got to head out to the auto shops to see about some work." Margaret climbs up on the bed.

"What happened last night?" Deliah rubs her eyes.

"Now, no drinking today."

"When will you be home?"

"Not too late."

She picks up Margaret and follows me to the door. "Whatever happened last night, Henry, I'm sorry."

"I'll be back for dinner." I pat Margaret on the head. I get my hat and coat and walk out.

* * *

I finally left. The squalor, the babies' cries and I'd find Deliah passed out on the floor, no meal made. Nothing. Beah could take care of me like a woman is supposed to do, and I could focus on my work, so I could do great things. A man needs to come home to a pretty smile and a warm meal. I had to leave Deliah, or she was going to take me down with her. No sir, I had places to go. I didn't go to trade school for nothing. I was building my reputation: people trusted me with their cars. Children, they'll get along. I got along when my mother left me at Aunt Julia's. Only the strong survive.

That's what my mama said, patting me on the back before she left. "Only the strong . . ." I was five when Aunt Julia took me in. I kept waiting for my mother to come and get me.

The creaking of Aunt Julia's rocking chair kept me up. I peeked through the crack in the curtain that separated the bed from the kitchen. "The boy is all alone in this world now, such a shame, such a shame," Aunt Julia sobbed.

"There, there, Julia, he has us, he has us now." Granduncle Isaiah's voice was unusually gentle.

"May the Lord forgive her, forgive her Jesus!" Aunt Julia held up her cross. "We'll tell him it was an accident. Right Isaiah?"

"Yes Julia, yes." Isaiah placed his hands on her shoulders.

"Losing her husband, too much, just too much for her. She done give up. That poor chile, jumping in front of a train . . ."

Who are they talking about? Who jumped in front of a train? My ears perked up.

"I'll tell Henry in the morning, after breakfast." The creaking stopped. Me? They were talking about me? My mama is gone? I tried not to imagine her body smashed by a train. I tried not to imagine her face, her eyes, her hands on my cheek. I forced myself to forget her. Heck, I was ten years old, going to be a man soon. I made myself forget her.

I was eating my morning biscuit when Aunt Julia sat at the table across from me and told me about the "accident." I took it like a man. I didn't cry, nope. I finished my breakfast, did my chores and walked to school with the boys.

MARGARET

Portland, Maine
1941

SILVER CUPS

I remember the song playing on the radio when my father left: *"The bells are ringing for me and my gal."*

My mother screaming at him in rage—the twins in saggy diapers crying, holding on to the edge of the crib. I stand next to them with eyes wide—my father tall, black, elegant.

"That's it, Deliah, that's it. I'm not going through this again." He reaches for his hat by the door.

Mother in a white slip holds a drink, swaying as she walks. "You can't leave me! You can't leave me here! I stopped singing for you—made you these babies—I could have toured with Ellington that night but I chose you, you!"

She drops her drink, falls to the floor and hugs his leg—like I wanted to, just like I wanted to do, no, Daddy, please don't go . . .

"Don't leave me, Henry, don't leave me. The children, what about the children, Henry?"

"You don't cook, you don't clean—this place is a dump—you just drink, drink! You're washed up!" He shakes his leg like he is shaking off a horrid creature.

My mother falls to the floor. "You can't leave me, you can't leave me, Henry, you can't leave—"

My father's face is calm and in control. "Now, Margaret, you take care of these boys." He nods his head, puts on his hat and leaves.

Mother throws her glass at the door. "You bastard! You're all alike, you're all alike!" Glass shatters, door shut, father gone. Twins crying, sagging diapers. I am five. My mother scans the room. I cower.

"It was you—you, Margaret, he left because of you, because you are a bad, bad ugly girl!" She staggers after me—I run and hide under the couch—

"You, come here! Come here!" She grabs for my limbs—I hide way in the back of the couch and press against the wall. Across the room, the twins wail so loud, enough to get her attention.

"Shut up!" She gets up. "Shut up shut up shut up!" She runs to them and I quickly roll out from under the couch. My mother lifts her hand to smack them—I stand between her and the crib as tall as I can be and she smacks me so hard, again and again—

"Shut up shut up shut up!" Until she is a pile on the floor again, the white slip, the shattered glass, the twins whimpering now. The radio still playing:

"The bells are ringing for me and my guy . . ."

In between my mother's cries, I can still decipher the melody.

I roll on my side; my back is sore from last night's beating. The twins are fussing in their cribs. Mother sweeps up the broken glass and changes the twin's diapers.

"Margaret, give these boys their bottles."

I slide off my bed, open the ice box and hand the twins their bottles. Their crying ceases as they suck hungrily. My tummy rumbles. "Mama, I'm hungry." I brace myself, afraid of what she will do.

"I can't do everything around here." Her lips press into a line. She washes out a dirty cup, pours milk into it and places it on the table. I don't move.

"So go on, Margaret, drink your milk. What are you expecting? To drink from a silver cup?"

I cautiously walk to the table. The twins peer at me above

their bottles. "Mama, what is silver?"

"Silver is something you will never drink out of; it is what rich people have. Rich children drink out of silver cups, like kings and queens. Now drink up, we don't want to be late for church."

Silver cups. I think of little girls and boys with crowns on their heads, sitting at a grand table drinking milk out of magnificent cups. "Lloyd and Hank, you are the princes, and I am the princess, see—see my silver cup?" I lift my chipped ceramic white cup and the twins raise their bottles. "Cheers!" I say as I bump my cup with their bottles.

"Jeers, jeers," Hank says, clicking his bottle against mine. "Jeers, jeers." They both laugh, banging their bottles.

"Put on your crowns," I command, pretending to put a crown on my head. "We are the rich children with crowns on our heads." The twins giggle. My mother appears, transformed from the white slip mound on the floor to a beauty dressed in her Sunday best: hat, coat, skirt, pumps, stockings, red lipstick and piercing eyes.

"Now come on, baby Lloyd." She picks him up, cradles him in her arms. "That's my baby." Lloyd, the color of coffee with cream, is my mother's favorite. Hank, the dark one, she leaves for me. She gently places Lloyd down, lifts Hank out of his chair and motions me to get him ready. She kisses Lloyd on the cheek; I do the same to Hank and get him dressed as Mother dotes on Lloyd. "Margaret, get your dress on, it's time to go."

I quickly put on my Sunday dress and buckle shoes. Hank clings to my legs.

We walk down the steps of our flat. My mother holds Lloyd and I take Hank's hand, trying to maneuver the stairs carefully. She pulls the stroller out of the garage and tucks the boys inside with a blanket. It's a cool, spring morning, winter gone for the moment; the air stings my nose. The tree in the lot beside our building has angry buds ready to burst. It's my tree, no one else's tree, only mine. I let go of Hank's hand and skip to the tree. I reach for one of the gray bare branches, swing my body back and forth and fall to the ground. Hank giggles.

"Come now Margaret, we don't want to be late," Mother says impatiently. Her heels click on the pavement as she pushes the stroller. We walk, a long way for me. Mother stops to light a cigarette. With each exhale she lets out a sigh—one hand pushing the stroller, the other hand clutching her cigarette.

We get to the church, the solemn building; Mother drops her cigarette and grinds it to the ground. "Come, children, let us light a candle for the Virgin Mary." People fill the pews; the priest stands in front of the great cross. Mother lights a candle. "Margaret, make a wish and the Virgin Mother will grant it."

I know what I want. I ask the Virgin Mother to please send us silver cups to drink so we can be like rich children, like kings and queens. The candle flickers. My mother kneels, crosses herself and enters the pew, and puts Lloyd on her lap. She gives him a pacifier and hands one to me, for Hank. I kneel and cross myself before entering, trying to emulate my mother's moves. I place the pacifier in Hank's mouth as he snuggles between Mother and me. Our neighbor Aunt Jo waves at me. I wave back and my tummy rumbles. The kids in the neighborhood call her Aunt Jo because she bakes cookies and gives them to us—that is, if we have been good boys and girls that go to church. Mother sits in a daze as the sermon begins, words mumbling out of the priest's mouth. I fall asleep dreaming of silver cups.

It smells in the apartment and every so often at night, a rat scurries by on the floor. It must be morning, I can't tell—all the blinds are drawn. A sliver of light pushes through the drab green curtains. Dust motes dance in the sun like snowflakes. My mother stumbles into the living room in her silk bathrobe, her hair in tangles, a drink in her hand.

"What are you looking at?" She shuffles, mumbling to

herself. "That's what happened. That's what happened, lost my chance to sing. Oh—I never told you how it happened, did I? Never did. I was a featured singer that night—I felt beautiful—I was beautiful. Your father sat in the audience, summer at Old Orchard Beach Pier. I wore a sequined beige dress that sparkled in the light like diamonds. Yes, a beauty! I was beautiful!" She takes a sip of her drink and spins around. "We were the opening act for the great Duke Ellington! The number I sang was 'I Got It Bad and That Ain't Good.' I did alright, I did—sang the words like I meant them. I didn't know the great Duke was in the audience, but he was, he was. Our time was up, I was leaving the stage and he stopped me—yes, the great Duke stopped me. He told me I sang pretty good and he invited me on tour with him! He gave me his card and your father took my hand and we danced that night to the beats of Ellington, danced all night . . ."

My mother sways back and forth dancing with an imaginary partner, with her drink. The rat runs past her and I quickly crawl up onto the sofa. I want to go outside and swing on my tree. I want to play with Hank and Lloyd. I don't dare move, I don't want to get hit. Mother keeps talking and I stay on the couch.

"We were in love!" She twirls around. "He was successful enough, educated, taught classes on auto mechanics, and fun, fun, fun—handsome—though Mama didn't care for him. Too black, she said, worried about what our kids would turn out like, not like me, light enough, 'cause of my Irish father—

"Oh Papa, Papa, he'd sing to me every night, he would." She sings to herself, real soft.

"Henry was going to take me away from there—the dirty distillery, barrels and bottles—he was going to make me his wife, take care of me. I was his wife, had his babies—your father, your father lied to me! My mother was right. I should not have trusted a dark Negro man. I could have gone on tour with Ellington. Your father told me he loved me, he was going to take care of me, take me away from that wretched home, smelly distillers . . .

"And I let him take me, I let him. I loved your father—Margaret, he lied. He left me to what, to what, Margaret? To this dump! This wretched stink hole and I could have been singing with the great, the greatest of the greats!" She hurls her drink against the door. She picks up the ashtray and throws it across the room. It hits the wall, shattering to pieces. Hank and Lloyd start to cry.

"Nobody cares about me anymore—nobody cares at all. Margaret, never trust them, they will lie to you." She holds my face in her hand. "All men do is take from you and offer skeletons in return—skeletons! Remember that, remember that!" She picks up a bottle off the floor, carries it like a baby and walks to her bedroom.

It's nighttime now. Mother is asleep in her room. Twins are whining, we are all hungry; there is no food. I walk into her room. She is passed out on the floor. I nudge her and she mumbles.

She opens one eye. "Is it morning? Time to go to church?"

"No, Mama, it's nighttime. We're hungry."

"Well, I'm sorry we don't have food. Your father did not leave us anything. Go ask Aunt Jo, go to Aunt Jo." She turns around and curls up like a baby.

I walk back to the living room; the twins reach out to me: "Mama, Mama . . ."

I tell them I'm going to get us something to eat. I pat them on their heads and walk out the door to Aunt Jo's. The streetlight is on; happy voices come from Aunt Jo's place. My mother says they are Italian. I decide I want to be Italian when I grow up. I knock on the door, no answer. I almost turn back. I don't want to interrupt the happy voices. My tummy rumbles. I knock again. Aunt Jo answers, brown hair pulled back, apron around a big tummy, jovial face and soft brown eyes.

"Yes, little one, what are you doing out alone?" She has a towel in her hand.

"My mother sent me."

"For what, child? My, you are a mess!" My nose is running and my hair is matted in tangles. I wipe my nose on my sleeve and I start crying and I can't stop. She presses me against her round warm body.

"There, there, what is it?"

"I'm hungry. My mother told me to come."

She pauses and shakes her head. "You just wait right here." I try and make out what Aunt Jo and the other adult voices are saying. My nose is running from all my crying. Aunt Jo comes back with a basket covered with a green cloth. "Now dear, you just take this basket up to your place. You can return the basket tomorrow. Here is a hanky, let me wipe that face. It's going to be okay, Margaret, God always provides."

"Thank you, Aunt Jo."

"God bless you, Margaret."

"God bless you, Aunt Jo."

She closes the door. I carry the basket up the stairs, into the apartment.

* * *

I come home from school excited about a new book in my bag to read to Hank and Lloyd. Skipping as I sing my ABCs, sirens interrupt my song. An older neighborhood boy with freckles walks by me with his friend, a shorter stubby version of him.

"What's that all about?" his friend asks.

"Oh, one of the nigger boys got hit by a truck."

"Huh." The stubby boy shrugs his shoulders and they walk by. I stop singing.

I run home and my mother stands in the apartment window waving Lloyd's shirt at me shouting, "Lloyd! Lloyd! Oh Margaret, it's Lloyd!" A truck is parked in the middle of the street in front of a small white blanket streaked with red. An ambulance and police cars with lights flashing surround my building. Hank sits on the steps dazed, holding a ball.

A skinny man talks to a policeman. "I didn't see him, I just didn't see him." He runs his hand through his thin hair.

My mother hurries down the stairs, "My baby, my baby!"

She runs toward the street, the policeman stops her. "Ma'am, I'm sorry, seeing him will only upset you further."

The policeman pulls her back. Mother wails. "My baby, my baby, let me see him—Lloyd! Lloyd!" She waves his shirt, heaving sobs into the policeman's arms. I sit next to Hank. His tiny hands squeeze the red ball to his chest.

Lloyd is a white lump with red streaks in the street. They take him in an ambulance but he's already dead. The policeman guides my mother up the stairs. She cradles Lloyd's shirt. "They were playing ball in the street, just playing ball, they always play ball in the street. Oh my Lloyd, my Lloyd!" The policeman motions us to go inside. Hank won't move.

"Come on, Hank," I say; he doesn't budge.

The officer lets go of my mother and bends down to Hank's face and tells him that if he comes inside he will get a lollipop. Hank nods and follows behind him. I want one too. The policeman searches his pocket and takes out two red lollipops for Hank and me. My mother sits down on the couch.

"You just stay here until your husband comes home, okay? And ma'am, I am sorry for your loss." The policeman tips his hat.

My mother mutters, "Officer, my husband is never coming home." She takes out a cigarette and lights it. I am grateful for the sweet taste of cherry in my mouth. Hank sucks on his lollipop and cuddles the ball. The policeman leaves and shuts the door.

Neighbors bring food for us and try to help my mother. She's making the funeral arrangements; I haven't been to school since the accident. Hank searches for Lloyd, I can tell. Hank is lost.

"He's in heaven now, Margaret, he's in heaven with Jesus." My mother has the phone to her ear.

"Yes, Mama," I say.

Mother talks into the phone. "Yes, I need to make arrangements for my little Lloyd, to be buried in the church cemetery. Yes, well, we are members of the church and Lloyd was baptized there. What? We're not allowed? Where am I going to bury my baby! Where? He needs to be put to rest! Don't tell me you're sorry! You're not sorry! He left me, it's not my fault, he left me!" My mother shrieks into the phone, bashing the receiver on the table over and over. "He left me! He left me!"

Mother doesn't hear the knock on the door. I open the door; it's Aunt Beah, her sister. "Oh dear, oh dear." She rushes to my mother. Beatrice is darker than Mother and fuller figured, with deep brown eyes. She smells of perfume and wears red lipstick. Her heels make a clicking sound on the floor as she passes me.

"Deliah, Dee." She takes the phone receiver out of her hand. "Dee, I'm so sorry, so sorry." She embraces her, and Mother almost disappears in her brown arms.

"They won't bury Lloyd, Beah, they won't bury Lloyd! Because I'm divorced!" Mother spits out her words. "Now where can he rest?" Where is Lloyd now? Is he lying in a crib until he can get to heaven? I want to see Lloyd again, I want to tickle him and make him laugh. I want to hold his chubby hands and read books to him.

Aunt Beah tells mother not to worry, that she will call the Episcopalian church down the street for Lloyd, then he can rest there. She tells me to put the kettle on for tea. I fill the kettle with water and put it on the stove. Aunt Beah says that God wanted Lloyd for some reason. She puts a saucer and tea cup in front of mother, "Lloyd will rest in peace. I promise."

Mother sinks down in her chair, waiting for tea.

At the Episcopalian church, we dress in black. Mother sits upright, her black hat and veil covering her eyes. My black patent shoes shine, and my dress is stiff. Hank pulls at the buttons on his black vest. The pew is hard. People come in, somber, to the sound of the organ. And there is Daddy, grander than ever with Aunt Beah by his side. She has her arm through his; I can see her red lips from my seat. I run to Daddy and put my face on his legs, hugging them.

"There, there, Margaret, you go and sit with your mother." He shoos me away. Aunt Beah smiles at me. Mother turns her head and her expression hardens. I sit back down. The preacher talks a long time. Mother occasionally wipes her eyes with her handkerchief. The preacher stops talking and people rise to view the tiny box in front.

Mother takes our hands. "It's time to say goodbye to Lloyd."

We walk to the front of the tiny box. Hank says, "Lloyd? Where's Lloyd?"

Mother pats his arm. "Hank, we are saying goodbye to Lloyd. He is going to heaven."

"Lloyd, Lloyd." Hank cries. She props Hank on her hip, the organ music rises. My mother leans over. Lloyd is faded and stiff like a doll. She kisses his forehead. Hank twists and turns in Mother's arms. "Lloyd, Lloyd!" As if trying to wake him, he keeps shouting, "Lloyd, Lloyd!"

Mother shushes him. "He's sleeping, shhh, he's sleeping." Lloyd is tucked in the box. I wonder if he's in heaven now.

In the graveyard behind the church, there is a small rectangle ditch in the ground. The June sun is still bright. We surround the ditch. The preacher stands behind it, deep lines in his forehead, holding an open bible. There's Daddy again, arm and arm with Aunt Beah. A tiny box is next to the ditch. That is Lloyd's box. My mother drops to her knees. "Not Lloyd, not Lloyd, not my baby!" Maybe they could take Lloyd out of the box to see if he might wake up. "No! No! Not Lloyd!" my mother cries. Aunt Beah and Daddy hurry over to her.

Aunt Beah touches Mama's shoulder. "Deliah, he's in heaven now, heaven."

My mother flicks Aunt Beah's hand away. "Don't talk to me about heaven, you whore! Couldn't wait to get to him, could you? You're nothing but a whore!" She starts to swing at Aunt Beah.

Aunt Beah moves back and Daddy comes between them. "Now, Deliah, calm down, calm down."

"Don't you tell me to calm down! It's your fault Lloyd died! Where were you, Henry? Where were you? In bed with her?" She gets up and pounds her fists on Daddy. He catches her wrists. "Let me go! Let me go!" she howls. I hold onto Hank's hand. All eyes are on Mother and not on the box. She falls to the ground, pulling out grass. "You should have been there, Henry, you should have been there. Our baby's gone, gone."

"I know, Deliah, I know." Daddy lifts her up as Lloyd's box is lowered into the ditch. "Only the strong survive now, Deliah, only the strong survive." Mother is broken in Daddy's arms, barely standing. Hank and I watch them cover the box with dirt and it disappears like a toy in the sand.

DELIAH

"It's a Blue World" is on the radio. I sing along, the babies are asleep. I open the window and inhale the damp, cool Portland air. Henry, Henry—I miss him, want him to embrace me, just hold me. I sing into the night, hoping my words will latch onto him somehow like a fish hook, to bring him home. Didn't he care even a little? How could he leave me like this? I sink into the words, throwing myself into them, longing . . . and down the street he's holding his hat. "Keep singing, Deliah, keep singing." My heart stops.

He walks up the stairs, I meet him at the door. He hangs up his hat and coat.

"I missed you, baby."

"You did?" I embrace him.

"Wrap your legs around me like you used to, baby." He takes me in his arms and carries me to the bedroom, places me on the bed and I try, I try to hold onto him, hold on. "These legs, baby, I missed these legs." And he enters me, all the emptiness I've felt, I longed for him to fill—

He lays limp on my chest, I squeeze his back tight. He brushes my hair from my face, and I start to cry. "Deliah, baby, Deliah, don't cry, don't cry."

"You left me, Henry, and what am I to do, what? I'll stop drinking for you, I will, I will." I lay my head on his black, smooth chest, run my fingers up and down across his shoulders, his strong arms. His chest, my home, I could rest on like I used to, and he'd stroke my hair. We'd lie like that, every second an eternity. "Didn't you ever think about me? Did you ever care?"

"I'm here aren't I? Now dry your tears and get my drink." He kisses me. I put on my robe, he pats my bottom. I bring him his drink, scotch on the rocks, lie down across his chest and fall asleep to his heartbeat. He doesn't stay. He places my head on the pillow, gets up and puts his clothes on.

"Henry, stay—Henry . . ."

"Deliah, I've got to go."

"Please, Henry, please? The children, Henry, think about Margaret and Hank. They need you." He buttons his shirt.

"Deliah, be good now." He walks out of the bedroom. I can't get up. I can't hold onto him. The emptiness creeps in again. I reach for the bottle on the dresser and drink myself to sleep.

Who am I? What am I? I'm nothing, no man loves me—though I take them to my room—they leave money on the dresser, that's how I survive. Got to take care of this throbbing headache, hungry children pestering me. Is it morning? Guess it is, sunlight too bright. Little Margaret opens the ice box, takes out milk for her and Hank. I put the kettle on for coffee and sit down staring into thick space. Hank breaks my gaze. "What do you want?" Margaret stands in front of Hank, guides him towards the door and they hurry out to school.

"Out of here! Out of here!" The door slams behind them. Where's that coffee? Where's—where's—? I fall to the kitchen floor cradling my achy head. "Where's Henry, where's . . . baby Lloyd?" Sun beams through the kitchen window, for a moment I feel grace, like the Virgin Mary herself touched me—

Why did you take him? Why did you take him? Why. Why, why my baby, my baby. The whistle of the kettle startles me. It must be Monday. I get up, turn the kettle off and make some coffee.

HENRY

.

Couldn't get her out of my head that night. My legs walking to her, stopping into bars along the way. Was that Deliah's voice? Heading up Munjoy Hill, street light spilling onto the ground, nodding to folks as I pass by. Confident by the sounds of my shoes hitting the pavement, expensive shoes only a successful man wears, yet I'm walking back, walking back. That's her voice, there she is singing just like I met her, the bird I captured, now in that apartment, that cage, that miserable cage. How I long for her again the way it was—she motions me to come up. The apartment is in shambles, clothes strewn about, bottles, shambles. I pick her up and carry her where I want, the bedroom. I need to feel Deliah's legs around me, need to feel Deliah's touch, need to feel Deliah. She embraces me, doesn't resist. "It's okay, baby, it's alright, your body is meant to be held. Come here, lie on my chest, let me hold you, baby. There there, sweet Deliah, world can't hurt you now, you're right in my arms, right where you need to be. Feeling your skin, soft and smooth, Deliah, my delight. We can lie like this forever, baby, like this forever."

"Take me, Henry, take me."

"Oh baby, baby." Those soft lips, those warm thighs. "Baby, you still do it for me, my delight, Deliah delight."

"Oh Henry." She pushes her breasts up for my mouth to meet, and I thrust inside her, all the while she's moaning, the backboard banging, just like the old days. The inevitable comes, the crying—here she goes, why did she have to go and ruin it for me? I placate her, although I know I need to leave before I'm trapped again, in this cage, and go home to my real woman, Beah, who takes care of me. Not like this place, she knows how to care for her man. Poor Deliah, she is a broken bird, she doesn't know how. I put her sleepy head on the pillow, get my clothes on, ignore her pleas, and leave with her scent on me.

MARGARET

In the summer of not Lloyd things got worse. I missed school, my teachers, the lunch and books. Books, books took me to faraway lands, far away from my mother's rage, the filth, the hunger pains. Lloyd left an empty hole in our apartment. Hank refused to sleep in the crib he used to share with Lloyd and curled up next to me at night.

I got good at guessing what mood my mother was in each morning. If she came out of her room shuffling her feet as if carrying something heavy, Hank and I were in trouble. We would scramble underneath the couch and wait for her to return to her room. If I misjudged her moods she'd go after Hank: "You were the one that was supposed to die, the dark one—you, Hank! Why didn't God take you?" I'd get in between her and Hank trying to protect Hank, my baby. It was my turn: "Margaret, you are a stupid ugly girl, that's why your Daddy left!" And the smacks came hard. Sometimes I'd run outside, down the steps to the back yard to my big oak tree, she wouldn't bother me there. I sang to my tree, silly songs I'd make up and it didn't mind me plucking some of its green shiny leaves. I'd pray to the tree for my Daddy to come back and bring lots of food and toys for me and Hank, and I could sit on his lap like I used to.

If she came out with quick light steps it was the nice mother, and she would tell me to hurry and get Hank dressed because we were going to church or to Lloyd's grave. There were days she did not come out at all. Hank and I had to fend for ourselves. I went to Aunt Jo and the nuns on Mercy Street, begging for food.

Sometimes men would come, strange men who would slip into our mother's bedroom, make all kinds of sounds. I tried to sleep, Hank and I tried to sleep. One time I woke to a monster's hands on my body down below, it was a monster, I tried to scream for help but a hand covered my mouth. I made myself frozen so the monster would leave. But he didn't. After that I'd see them come up the stairs and I'd pull Hank's hand and we'd run down the stairs and climb my tree. We'd stay there sitting on the thick gray branch till the men left, counting stars till late at night.

I decided I would be a nun when I grew up. I would help all the poor children that needed help. The nuns were safe in the church. God loved them best because they gave up their lives for him and wore habits.

Daddy was going to visit us. Mother cleaned, cooked and made sure we were bathed and ready—most of the time, he didn't show. One night, Hank and I waited all night for him, hoping the door would open—it never did. When Daddy did come, he'd hold me in his lap and whisper I was his favorite. He'd sing silly songs to me and Hank. He had a new family with Aunt Beah, a boy, Kenny.

That summer was a hungry summer that went into a hungry winter. That winter the United States declared war on Germany. We had our own war going on, trying to be fed, trying not to get hit, trying to find warmth—the nuns—if it weren't for the nuns Hank and I would have starved. I begged because I had to. Hank depended on me.

DELIAH

1944

"You look like Clark Gable. Do you know that? Hey, bartender, get a drink for the movie star here."

I stumble towards the bar, he gently takes my arm to steady me and whispers in my ear, "You sing like an angel."

"Oh you liked it? Well in that case, bartender, two drinks!" I take out a cigarette, he gives me a light, my eyes steady on him a little, his olive skin, thin mustache and gentle brown eyes. I wonder how much money he'll leave me. He takes his drink and pushes mine aside. "Who you think you saving that for?" I slide it back to me.

"You've had enough already." His broad shoulders block me; I place my palms on his chest.

"Why you doing that?" I take his drink from his hand and head toward the stairs. I glance behind my shoulder.

"Where are you going?" He wipes his forehead with his handkerchief. I lift my dress slowly as I walk up the stairs, feeling his eyes on the back of my legs, my thighs. He follows me into the room. The band starts the second set, the crowd swings to the beat.

I sit on the edge of the bed: cigarette in one hand, drink in the other. "So, what will it be?"

"What do you mean?" He is dumbfounded. It must be his first time, I have to spell it out for him.

"How do you want it?" I finish my drink. What does this man want? This is going to be a long night.

"I don't even know your name." Name? Name? What does my name have to do with anything? I'm gonna need another drink to get through this one. I plaster on a smile.

"Coy, hard to get? You seem that type." I put out my cigarette.

"There seems to be a misunderstanding." He stands in front of me. Should I yell for Eva? Is this guy up to no good? "What's your name, darling?"

"Darling?" I wait for him to make a move, he doesn't.

"Yes, darling, what's your name?"

Something catches in my throat. "Deliah."

"Deliah, I'm taking you away from this place." He's trying to blow my cover, I can't look at his face. Now he knows my name, how do I play this one?

"Why?" His shoes are shiny brown leather, with short laces. They are respectable shoes that only a respectable man wears. What on earth does he want with me?

"You are too good for this, come on now." He takes my arm and leads me out the door. Maybe this man really is Clark Gable. He navigates us through the dance floor, moving in between dancing couples, not missing a syncopated beat.

It's misty outside, I feel dizzy, his arms anchor me as we walk to his car. He opens the door for me. I obediently get in, wait a minute what am I doing? He starts the car. I touch his hand—"Wait, what's your name?"

"Batch."

"Batch?"

"Yes."

"Batch, where are you taking me?"

"Home, darling, I'm taking you home. Where is it?" I give him my address and he speeds down the street. Why is he going so fast? I haven't cleaned the place in months, and the children, who knows what they'll be into. Shame creeps over me.

He parks the car on the side of the road and lights a cigarette. "You no longer have to do that anymore."

"Why?"

"Because I'm here now. I'm going to take care of you."

I drop my head into my hands.

"What, what's wrong?" He touches my back.

"I'm a damn mess, a mess!" I start pulling at my hair.

"Shh, shh, I'm here now."

"You can't come up, the children . . . the place . . ." He hands
me a handkerchief. I dry my eyes.

"I'll come by in the morning to check on you. Okay, Deliah?"

Is he for real? Maybe I drank too much. He walks around
the car, opens the door for me and takes my hand like I'm
Queen Victoria. Hah! He's bluffing, what angle is he playing?
He doesn't kiss me goodnight. He waits until I walk up the steps
to my door, tips his hat and gets in his car. I wave as it glides
down the wet street and turns the corner.

MARGARET

I'm a big girl now. Hank and I walk to school every day. He's in the first grade; I am in third. Sometimes the teacher tells me he acts up in class and the teacher asks him, "Why can't you be like your sister Margaret?" I tell his teacher he will do better and scold Hank and tell him to be a good boy. I am a good girl. That's what the teacher tells me.

Sometimes the other children make fun of my hair because it is extra curly. I say quit it because I'm Italian but they don't believe me. Mother says they are ignorant. The people that call us niggers are ignorant, she says.

We have a new daddy; we call him Papa Batch. He has light brown skin and a skinny mustache like Clark Gable. He makes me and Hank laugh and calls us names like "banana head" and "strawberry head." We laugh and make him call us other fruit names. Papa Batch is Portuguese. He is quiet, especially when the angry mother comes out. He usually leaves and comes back later.

My daddy left Aunt Beah and has another family. He comes to visit sometimes in a fancy car that he made. I don't know the names of his new family. We have a new baby; her name is Francine. She is light like a doll. Mother doesn't like her crying. Mother flies after her—one time I had to stop her from banging baby Francine against the wall. Mother still has her moods, even with Papa Batch, but we aren't hungry anymore. Maybe if I stop

Mother from hurting baby Francine, Papa Batch will stay. I want Papa Batch to stay.

I like to sing. I place my books on the end table by the couch singing a new song I learned at school. Baby Francine is in her crib; she rarely leaves it.

Mother shuffles into the living room in a robe. "Margaret, is that you singing?"

"Yes, I learned a new song at school!"

"Oh, so you think you can sing, Margaret?" She bends down, pointing her finger in my face. I can smell the alcohol. "You can't sing, Margaret, you are a terrible singer! You will never be a singer!" She slaps me so hard I fly across the floor. Baby Francine starts crying in her crib.

"Not you again!" Mother scowls. "Now Margaret, look what you've done, made the baby cry." She begins to slap baby Francine.

I get up and try to stop her. "No, Mother, no, no, stop!" The door opens; it is Papa Batch. Mother freezes.

"Darling, what's wrong?" Papa Batch steps inside and hangs up his hat. "Why is the baby crying? I brought some groceries."

Mother trembles. "It was her fault it was her fault it was her fault," she whispers. I wipe my nose. It's bleeding. Baby Francine whimpers.

"You've been drinking again, haven't you? You told me you were going to stop. Get back to your bed and sleep this off." She obeys like a child and goes to her room. Papa Batch tousles my hair and brings the groceries into the kitchen. I never sing in the house again.

DELIAH

It wasn't his baby, he knew—although he treated Francine like she was—and I got pregnant, his baby, his child—he made sure I didn't drink, said it wasn't good for the baby. Baby Francine, she was a mistake, not sure whose she was, went to confession for it, did a hundred hail Marys—God forgive me—Jesus forgive me . . .

Batch told me to sleep it off. Can't sleep, can't sleep—Goddamn, why is my hand shaking? I need a drink. Someone get me a drink around here! I bang on the door. "Batch! Batch! I'll be good I'll be good I promise I'll be good! Please just one drink, one—Batch, open the door!" Nobody's listening to me nobody—

I can't stop shaking—I'm being punished for all my sins—Francine isn't his baby, he knows that, I'm being punished for Francine—it was one of those men—I don't know who—one of them.

"Batch! Just a little one, a little one!" I bang again, he's at the door! "Please, baby, I'm in an awful way, a terrible way right now, please!"

"Darling, it's not good for the baby. Now calm down, sweetheart, and go to bed."

"Baby? Baby? Lloyd is dead, Henry, do you hear me, baby Lloyd is dead!"

"Shhh . . . shhh, it's okay, Deliah. Darling, go to sleep. It's late." He switches the light off.

"No, Batch, no, no!"

Where am I? Mama's kitchen, she's peeling potatoes, and Papa's there—sing me a song, Papa . . .

Please, Papa, sing me a song.

He found me on the floor in the morning drenched in sweat. I tried to stop drinking for his baby, baby Frances, I tried, but every so often, I'd sneak some, just a little.

MARGARET

Mother's belly is growing another baby inside. This time Papa Batch makes sure Mother doesn't drink so much. He says it's not good for the baby. Francine is different. She stares a lot and doesn't play like Hank and Lloyd used to.

Aunt Beah visits with her boys Kenny and Sammy. Mother and Aunt Beah sit at the kitchen table smoking cigarettes and drinking coffee, whispering to each other. Aunt Beah tells me to keep an eye on the children. I go to the living room and keep an ear open to the kitchen.

"He just up and left me too, with two boys." Aunt Beah laughs. "I'm glad I've got a job at the plant, got to help get those Germans, and it pays pretty good."

"I could have told you he would leave."

"He swept me off my feet, drove me in that car of his."

"Who is his new woman?" Mother asks.

"Julie Fletcher. I guess he got tired of me."

"Both of us." Aunt Beah and Mother cackle.

"Have you seen Mama recently?" Mother asks.

"She's getting along, stubborn as ever, still making that moonshine."

"That's what got me started."

"Getting older you know, slower, doesn't talk much, doesn't care much for my boys."

Silence falls between them. Cigarette smoke swirls above, hanging onto the space of unspoken words.

Kenny, Sammy, and Hank want to play ball outside.

"Come on, Hank!" Sammy, the youngest, bounces around the apartment impatiently. Hank tries to get the ball from Kenny.

"Wait, Sammy, let's see if Francine wants to play," Kenny says.

"She's not gonna wanna play, Kenny. Come on, Sammy." Hank takes the ball and runs down the stairs with Sammy.

Kenny walks to the crib and points to Francine. "Why is she in there?" Francine is rocking back and forth. "Isn't she too big to be in a baby crib?" Kenny asks me. He has big brown eyes and is dark, like our father. I feel embarrassed about Francine; she is too big for the crib. She's seven and she still likes it. She will spend hours in there hugging her favorite doll, Pudding. He peers over the crib. "Francine, do you want to come out and play ball?" She rocks back and forth squeezing Pudding. Kenny joins the game outside in the street. Their voices blend with feet pounding on the pavement. The sun is about to drop out of the sky, leaving a brilliant pallet of colors. I sit on the couch next to Francine as the light fades to the sound of her gentle rocking.

* * *

1953

After communion, I look for Father Joseph to ask him about becoming a nun. I knock timidly on the thick wooden door of the rectory.

"Come in." I open the door. "Oh, yes, Margaret, what brings you here?" I start to perspire.

"Yes, my child?" He sits at his desk, still in his robes from the service. I muster up the courage to speak.

"I would like to know how to become a nun." My hands are clammy. I wipe them on the side of my skirt.

"To enter the sisterhood? Margaret, that is a noble thought

of the highest order. Have you thought deeply about this?"

"Yes, Father. I want to serve God." I hold my cross necklace for strength.

"Margaret, there are many ways of serving the Lord. And you are so young, with your whole life ahead of you, with so much promise." My eyes start to tear up, and I can't stop it.

"Child, child, shh, shh, here now." He hands me a tissue. "Now, now, there are many ways to be on God's path, a beautiful young girl like you should think about settling down, having children. Margaret, you will make a wonderful wife and mother." I let go of my cross.

I leave despondent and walk home with my hands in my pockets and head down. I need another plan, I need to get away. I'm a good student, not like Hank. Poor Hank, his grades are tumbling down and he can't play football. I asked the coach to please give him another chance; he wouldn't, said the rules are the rules. Now, the rules are the rules and I can't be a nun. I thought God called me to do his work, and I was wrong. I don't know what to do now. I don't know what Hank will do.

The wind picks up. Is a storm coming? A huge shadow casts over me as a majestic bird circles above. The eagle circles around and around and into the horizon. You don't see eagles come this way, ever. This must be a sign from God telling me I will be alright, that everything will be alright.

"Take me to the water, Margaret." My mother is trying to get sober again. This time Batch said he will leave her if she doesn't stop drinking. Sometimes she trembles uncontrollably, and she smokes all the time. I'm a little anxious taking my mother out in her volatile condition. Batch taught me to drive in his gray Ford, I'm a good driver. My mother doesn't ever drive. She gives me the keys to Batch's car and we get in.

"Old Orchard Beach," she says in between puffing her cigarette. It's a short ride from Portland and I park on a side street near the pier. The pier extends out into the bay with the grand ballroom at the end where concerts are held. "This is where it all began. I sang here, Margaret, you know." Families and couples purchase tickets for rides and wait in lines for ice cream, cotton candy, lobster rolls, and fried clams.

"Yes, Mother, I know. You have told me many times how you met Duke Ellington." My friends and I come here often. My favorite ride is the Ferris wheel at sunset, where I'm suspended in the sky as the sun goes down and the moon appears before my eyes. She finishes her cigarette, flicks it on the ground and extinguishes it with her shoe.

"I need to see the ocean," she says, so we walk off the sidewalk into the sand. I take my shoes off; the sand is warm and comforting. We sit on a bench facing the water. The tide is coming in; the waves roll onto shore longer and stronger. "In Brunswick, we lived by a bay, with other Indian families. I sure ate a lot of fish back then, and I'd pray as a little girl to the bay every day to bring back my papa. You never met him. He died from drinking." My mother's tone is solemn. "I know I've made a terrible mess of things, and I'm sorry, Margaret. I'm sorry I've been, well, a terrible mother." She lights a cigarette. I'm not sure what to say. It's too late now. Francine is irrevocably damaged and Hank is going down a path I can't stop. I don't know what I'll do now that I won't be a nun. All I know is that I need to get out away from everyone I can't save.

"God forgives you." I manage to respond.

"Yes, Margaret, he does." She crosses herself.

I'm in a dreary mood as I walk down the hall from my last class to head home. I'm still trying to piece together my future. Chin up, Margaret, keep your chin up.

"Margaret!" My friend Isabella calls after me and hooks her arm in mine. "Where are you off to?"

"I'm just heading home." I unhook my arm.

"Come with me—I'm meeting the gang at Wally's for ice cream."

"Oh, I don't know . . ." Isabella is always full of pep. I envy her carefree manner. My shoulders are heavy and overburdened.

"Come on, Margaret, it will be swell." Her expression changes to concern. "What's wrong?"

"Father Joseph says I shouldn't become a nun, that there are other ways of serving the Lord and that I will make a good mother and wife."

"Well, darling, you will, you truly will!" She squeezes my arm.

"I need to have a plan, I had one, to join the sisterhood and now, I'm stuck, I will be stuck." Flashes of Francine rocking in her crib cowering in fear around Mother, and Hank, slipping away, hanging out with boys that smoke and race cars, overwhelm me. What will become of them? What will become of me? How can I get away? Isabella takes my hand and we sit down on top of the steps at our school's entrance.

"Come, Margaret." She hugs me and I rest my head on her shoulder.

"Oh Isabella! I had a plan—what will I do now? What? I can't stay at home any longer, I just can't . . ."

"Margaret, here." She hands me a handkerchief. "Why don't you apply to nursing school with me, Jody, and Anna? Just imagine all of us in Boston together—it will be grand!" Nursing school. A nurse. That is serving people too, but what about the cost?

"Oh, I don't know, that sounds expensive." I sigh. Isabella reassures me, that I am sure to get a scholarship. I start to feel a bit of hope. Isabella smiles and pats my arm.

"Now let's get some ice cream to celebrate!" She helps me up, we hook elbows and jog down the stairs and onto the street. I suppose nursing school is possible.

FRANCINE

Baby pudding baby pudding be a good baby good baby. No no no don't do that don't do that baby pudding I told you to stop stop—
    Shutupshutupshutupshutup
    Bad baby bad baby
       twinkle twinkle little star how I wonder what you are
    I said shutupshutupshutup
    twinkle twinkle—
    shutupshutupshutup
    baby pudding come here come here
    no I don't want to go outside and play no no no no Margaret, Margaret baby pudding being bad bad Margaret Margaret don't let Mama come again don't let
    above the world so high like a diamond in the—
    she's coming she's coming Margaret, Margaret where are you?

PART II

R.J.

BROWN SWAN

"R.J., you coming with us?" Kurt peeks into my room dressed in a suit, hat, and polished shoes, a handkerchief in his pocket.

"Don't know, Kurt. Where are you boys going?" I lift my head up from my book, half interested.

"A mixer, big band, girls, lots of girls. Come on, R.J., you work too hard." He snatches the book from my hands.

"I need to mark my page." I take the book back and fold a page corner. "Okay, Kurt, give me five minutes."

He tips his hat. "That's all you got, R.J." He shuts the door. Girls. Pretty girls. Been a long time, guess it's about time to go out.

We pile into Kurt's car—goddamn, why do they have to smoke? I rub my eyes. "Open the window please." I straighten my tie.

"Next thing you know you'll say I'm driving too fast," Kurt retorts.

"Come on R.J., loosen up." Danny ruffles my hair and Kurt laughs.

"Hey, Danny, cut the crap!" I smooth my hair back.

Jeff pulls out a flask. "Want some?"

"Sure, sure." I take a swig. Jeff never says much, keeps to himself and drinks a lot. I wonder how he's getting through his doctorate. The boys jump out of the car as soon as it's parked, and we swagger into the hotel lobby together, in search of the ballroom. The noise is unbearable, a mixture of loud voices and screeching horns. I head for the bar and let the fellows pass ahead of me. I order a beer, it's not cold enough, lukewarm. Jesus Christ! Can't they serve a decent beer here? I paid enough for it. I finish it anyways and slam the money down on the bar. No tip. I spot the boys sitting at a table gawking at the girls on the dance floor. Dancers with gyrating limbs flail about to the shrill horns and banging drums; my head is pounding. I'm about to leave—I spot her: brown skin against cream taffeta, large eyes, round hips, and full bosom. Her arms and legs move so fast she is a blur of cream and brown. I can't take my eyes off this creature, this brown swan. Am I standing straight? I am, I'm upright.

"Hey, R.J." Kurt slaps my back. "You star struck?"

Danny chimes in. "Like you've never seen a woman before."

"Danny, we all know you're a virgin, so back off." I smirk. Jeff and Kurt laugh. The radiant, brown, cream creature glides off the dance floor and joins a table of girls.

Kurt nudges me. "Why do you want her? She's colored. Or maybe you like them like that? Listen, R.J., I dare you five bucks to go over there and talk to her." He slaps a five on the table.

"Five bucks he won't do it," Danny counters. Jeff takes a swig of his flask. I don't even hear them, I don't hear anything, all I know is that I must meet this graceful girl. I walk as erect as possible, gripping onto my hat as perspiration collects in my hands. What am I going to say? Come on, R.J., think quick, think quick. I approach the table where the girls are chatting and applying lipstick. They turn their heads towards me.

"Good evening, ladies. May I ask where you are from?" I address the brown swan. She has a gentle gaze, and answers with a slight smile. "Why, we are from Boston University, Nursing School." Her voice is rich and deep, puts a sort of ease in me; I don't quite understand it. "What are your affiliations?"

"I am at Harvard, finishing up a doctorate in Engineering. My friends are over there."

"Oh, I see." She straightens her back a bit.

"My name is R.J., and you are?"

"Margaret. Pleased to meet you."

She takes my hand. "Do you know this song?"

"No, don't know it."

She jumps up and down, clapping her hands. "One of my favorite songs: 'Old Black Magic.' Frank Sinatra sings it, oh you must know him!"

"Yes, yes, of course."

"Aren't you going to ask me to dance?"

I can't resist her. I haven't danced since high school. I straighten my back as much as possible and take her hand. Somehow, we manage to move across the floor with the other dancers. The singer croons into the mic. Margaret sings along, smiling at me.

She wears a gold cross around her neck. A Catholic and colored. My mama would have a fit. Well, I'm far away from Arkansas. I went as far away as I could. Margaret certainly has me in a spell. Yes, she sure does.

The song ends; as we walk back to her table, I muster enough confidence to ask to see her again: "Margaret, it was a pleasure meeting you, and I hope that you may find time to meet with me again?"

She smiles demurely at me. "Why yes, R.J., I'd be happy to meet you again."

"Here, let me give you my number." I scrawl my phone number on the closest cocktail napkin and hand it to her.

"Why thank you." She puts the napkin in her purse and snaps it shut. There is something about her, the soft cadence of her speech; her unaffected grace stuns me and calms me simultaneously. She glances up at me, catching my unabashed stare, and smiles. "I very much enjoyed meeting you, R.J., thank you for the lovely time." She offers her hand. I take it; I can feel her warmth through her white satin glove.

"Please call me, Margaret." She nods her head and joins her group of friends at their table. Beads of sweat form on my forehead. I sure hope she calls me. I dab my forehead with my handkerchief, and the fellows greet me in their usual demeanor.

"Looks like R.J. got lucky." Kurt pats my back.

"If you call getting a colored girl lucky." Danny glowers at me. Jeff says nothing.

"You guys are a bunch of bastards!" I take the five-dollar bill off the table, walk out of the hall, and hail a cab home.

* * *

I'm playing in the yard with Sarah, my Negro friend. We are playing house. She pretends sticks are forks and knives. We are eating supper and my mama calls me in. "Robert James, come in and wash up, we are going to a picnic." My hands are brown, covered with dirt. I say goodbye to Sarah. She frowns, carrying sticks in her hands.

"We'll play tomorrow, Sarah." She drops the sticks and kicks the dirt with her bare feet, pouting her lips. She stomps off. In the kitchen, Mama flits about putting sandwiches in a basket. My father sits in his chair in the living room with a pipe in his mouth listening to the radio:

"Howdy! Coming to you from Hot Springs Arkansas your favorite hillbillies, Lum and Abner, brought to you by Quaker Oats; it's richer than other oatmeal."

Lum and Abner are funny, I want to stay and listen to the show. Mama asks me to carry the jug of lemonade. My father turns off the radio and gets his hat, my little brother hangs onto Mama's leg. We head to the open field not far from our house. There is an eerie jubilation in the street as people walk with their families to the picnic.

I wish I was back playing with Sarah. My mama seems

agitated and excited, my father his usual cheerless self.

"Why hello there, Maribelle, a nice day for a picnic isn't it?" Our neighbor Ellen twirls her parasol and smiles brightly at Mama.

"Why yes, it is, Ellen, nice to see you today," Mama replies graciously.

"We are going to try and get a good seat this time, so we can get a good viewing."

"Oh yes, we'll see you there," Mama responds as they stroll ahead of us. I trail behind Mama. The jug is getting heavy, I'm careful not to spill it though. I don't want a beating today.

Papa says menacingly, "Careful with the jug, boy!" I make my back as straight as I can and carry the jug in front of me, nothing spilled yet.

At the field, people gather around a tree. I can't see above them; there is a lot of commotion. "Get that nigger!" The crowd gasps and shouts. "That'll teach you looking at our women!" Another gasp, a groan. I peer through the people standing in front of me. There's a black man, eyes wide with terror, hands and feet bound, propped up against the tree. Men kick him, children throw rocks, people hurl insults and the crowd responds with glee. "Let's get this picnic started!" a man hollers. He's our neighbor, a big burly man with a long mustache. I never cared for him.

Two other men seize the Negro while my neighbor puts a noose around his neck. They prop him up on a barrel for everyone to view. The crowd yells, "One, two, three!" and one of the men pushes him off the barrel and his body swings and jerks until it stops and his head slumps to the side. The crack, like a branch snapping in two, gets the crowd cheering. Men charge towards the body with knives and tear into his flesh, blood stains the grass below the tree. Boys, some I go to school with, yelp with glee, stab at the body with their pocket knives as it swings back and forth in the wind. A man pours liquid all over the body and lights a match. The air smells heavy with petrol and a sweet sickening smell of burning flesh.

"R.J., R.J., it's time to eat." Mama hands me a sandwich. She gingerly smooths out the blanket. I hold the sandwich in my hand and throw up in the grass, and I can't stop.

"What's wrong with him?" my father asks in his dry tone. My little brother bawls.

"Probably just all the excitement—he'll be okay." My mother places her hand on my back as I heave into the grass.

I can't move I can't move—frozen, can't breathe, what is that putrid smell? Sick sweet sick burning—I'm sweating. I had that nightmare again and can't get the swinging body out of my head.

MARGARET

He has blue eyes like Paul Newman. That's the first thing I notice about him—and his courteous manner, I believe from his southern upbringing, is almost stilted yet refreshing. He isn't much taller than me and has a slight hunchback. His blond hair is thinning a bit at the top. He wears it slicked back, which gives him a boyish appearance.

I ride the T to Boston Commons for our first date. It's a brisk fall afternoon; I'm glad I have on my red peacoat and gloves. We are meeting at the swan lake. I spot him at a distance, checking his watch. I wave to him; he grins and walks towards me. His gait is uneven, like he may have a strained back.

"Thank you, Margaret, for coming," he says in his slight southern accent.

"My pleasure, I hope I wasn't too late."

"Not too late, no. You're mighty pretty."

I smile.

"I thought we could take a nice walk through the Commons and head for a café on Newbury Street." He takes my arm, guiding me down the path to the Commons. We stop at a bridge. Below us tourists ride in swan boats on the pond.

"Sounds lovely. Oh, swans! So graceful." A group glides by, dipping their beaks into the water. They create circular patterns that ripple and extend into the lake.

"Yes, just like you."

I blush. "R.J., where are you from?"

"Arkansas. I left as soon as I could. After undergrad school I came up here."

"Well, it's quite different here I imagine."

"Yes. And it is a changing world. Margaret, where is your family from?"

"Portland, Maine."

"Where are they originally from?"

"My father is Negro and my mother is American Indian, Irish, and Negro. So, I suppose I am American."

"Yes, I suppose you are."

"Is that troubling for you?" I hold onto the railing.

"What?"

"That I am colored?"

"No, Margaret, no. I never understood the division; growing up in the South no one could ever explain why we had to be separate, why I could no longer play with my Negro friend after a certain age. We all lived together and there were rules and we followed them. But I never understood them and I still don't."

"You know interracial marriage is forbidden in the southern states."

"Yes. I believe there is opportunity here in the North to promote change." An older woman scatters breadcrumbs from the bridge. A swan curves its neck into half a heart shape and daintily pecks at the crumb. The water reflects a mirror image of a whole heart. The swan lifts its neck and it is gone.

"Yes, I hope so." We walk in silence for a bit. He stops and adjusts his back. "Does your back hurt, R.J.?"

"Well no, it's the result of a bad birth. Somewhat of an injury."

"Oh my, what happened?"

"My mama almost died, and they had to pull me out with forceps. Smashed up my head real good. And it turns out, later on, I was unable to walk. One leg grew longer than the other.

So, I had to have surgery. I was about two or so. And the only doctor was in Texas, so my mama and papa drove me to the hospital in Texas and they dropped me off. I was there for quite a while, months, crying for them every day, until, well, I just gave up. I was in a body cast for months. They had to cut into my leg and shorten the bone so my legs would grow at the same rate. I couldn't move. My parents came back for me, and I didn't know who they were. The smell of ether to this day makes me faint." He chuckles.

"That must have been so difficult. I've cared for children after serious operations, and some did not make it." I hold my cross. Those poor little ones, bless their souls. "Did the surgery work?"

"Yes and no. I had to teach myself to walk. My papa was too busy at his auto shop and my mama upkeeping the house, and she was pregnant at the time. I still have trouble, can't differentiate up from down. I have to think about it. Though I've gotten along."

"Yes, I would say you have. Ph.D. from Harvard, quite impressive. I would like to get a Ph.D. too."

"Really?" He raises his eyebrows in disbelief.

"Yes, someday." I smile at him.

It is a delightful café on Newbury street, crowded with couples and families enjoying the sunny afternoon. I order a tuna salad and he orders a hamburger and beer. We hold hands across the table. "You know, Margaret, I want to settle down." His tone is serious.

"Me, too." I squeeze his hand. The waiter, a handsome Negro man, carefully places the plates in front of us. I'm famished. R.J. takes a bite of his burger.

"Damn it!" He irately puts his burger down on his plate.

"What's wrong?" I'm a bit startled by his sudden outburst.

"I said medium rare and there is nothing rare about this

burger. Where is the waiter?" He waves his hand, trying to get the waiter's attention. He is about to explode.

"It's okay, R.J., they can fix it." I pat his arm and he briskly shoves my hand away.

"I told him medium rare! Didn't you hear me say medium rare?" He motions the waiter over and gives him a tongue lashing: "Why is my burger medium? I told you I wanted my burger medium rare. Do you know the difference between medium and rare?" The man's face is stolid, like a mask. I can tell he is holding back.

"Clearly it was just a mistake and they can make you another burger, R.J." The waiter glimpses at me for an instant. Can he tell I am part black? He reminds me of my brother Kenny: tall, dark skin and a prominent nose.

"This is ridiculous!" R.J. throws his napkin down on his plate. Heat rises in my throat. I take a sip of water. Patrons around us frown and whisper.

"Here, R.J., have some water." I move his glass closer to him.

"I want to know if you know the difference between rare and medium!"

"R.J., calm down. He will bring you another burger, it was a mistake."

"I pay good money and I expect to receive good service! Damn ni—"

"R.J., what? Damn what?" I throw my napkin down. "R.J. say it—what were you going to say?" R.J.'s face is red with rage.

The white manager comes over to our table. "Sir, what seems to be the problem?"

R.J. smiles graciously and whispers to the manager. "It appears that this boy does not know the difference between medium and rare. I clearly ordered a medium rare burger, and this burger is not rare at all."

"Sir, we will certainly make you another burger—free of charge. My apologies." He motions the server to take the plate.

The waiter complies quickly and walks to the kitchen.

R.J. adjusts his tie and wipes his forehead with his hand-kerchief. He attempts to regain his geniality. "Margaret, how is your salad?"

"What were you going to say, R.J.? Why don't you just say it?" I gather my clutch purse and peacoat.

"Margaret, please sit down. Please. I am sorry to be so troublesome. Sometimes my upbringing just slips out. Please, Margaret, please allow me one more chance?" He pulls out my chair for me. The manager chastises the waiter in the back of the café.

"I'm sorry, Margaret." He hangs his head like a guilty child. I feel sorry for him. His blue eyes beckon me to sit, and I do, I sit back down.

"I suppose we can finish lunch."

Great relief spreads over his face. "Yes, let's forget the whole thing and enjoy our lunch. I know, why don't we start over?"

"We can try. Would you like some salad?"

"Why yes, that is very kind of you."

I place some salad on a butter plate and serve it to him and we enjoy the rest of lunch.

Before we leave, I take out a few dollars. "For your trouble . . . I'm awfully sorry for his behavior."

"It's not you that needs to apologize." The waiter hands me back the bills and I follow R.J. out of the café.

Sometimes he'd have flare ups and lose his temper, but it wasn't much. Besides, he asked me to marry him and I said yes. I know he will provide for me. My mother met R.J. and she pleaded with me not to marry him. "There is something off about him" she said. Imagine, my mother telling me someone was "off." I am glad for her, though. She is sober now and started an Alcoholics Anonymous group for women in Portland, the first of its kind. "Margaret," she said, "If you ever need help, you can come to me." It's hard to believe how much sobriety has changed her.

She's not the violent mother I grew up with. That's all in the past now, and I'm stepping into my future. I wish she could be happy for me. We've set the wedding date.

R.J.

Mama refused to come on the account that I was to marry a colored woman and a devout Catholic; her Baptist religion could only forgive so much. Neither my father nor my brother cared for coloreds. So, my family is not here. Kurt is my best man, though I don't really like him much either. We got a nice church in Boston, not too expensive, just right.

My granddaddy is probably rolling in his grave. He had slaves, just a few to help on the farm. He was good to them during Reconstruction: he kept them on as sharecroppers. And my mother, well, there are rules in the South to follow and you just don't cross over the lines in the minds of most people.

My mother grew up in Texas, and they were well off, educated compared to my father. Mama was a school teacher; she met Papa and he put an end to that. "No more teaching, you're my wife now." Papa dropped out of school during the Depression and he never got over it. His family didn't have the money to carry him through his studies. He owned an auto shop and made sure I could work as soon as I was able. We always had food on the table, but nothing extra. He was a bitter man and that Depression stayed inside him the rest of his life. He didn't help me at all. I had to work to get through my undergrad studies. I worked as a waiter, sold encyclopedias, and anything else to get buy. Here I am thirty-five and finally getting my Ph.D. My father doesn't talk to me anymore, he says we have nothing in common, now that I'm educated.

Margaret and I both agreed we wouldn't travel to the South. I didn't want to go back, and now it'd be dangerous if we did. I never thought I'd marry a colored woman, and here I am. I never thought I would meet someone like Margaret, and here she is.

I do.

I do.

MARGARET

Wayland, Massachusetts
1970

SPILLED MILK

The table is set. Five silver cups full of milk. Hot dogs, peas and corn scatter the children's plates like modern art. He sits at the end of the table, tight lips and tired eyes.

"What's for dinner, Margaret?"

"Lamb chops." I place a plate in front of him. The children squirm in their seats like worms.

"Sit still and eat," he commands.

"Time to eat, no more playing," I say softly. The three eldest carefully pluck at their food. The two youngest, Ella and Claude, are tickling each other, laughing, and it happens—Claude's cup turns over.

"I told you to stop fooling around! Look what you've done!"

"It's okay, R.J., I'll clean it up. It's just a little spill."

"Who did it?" he growls at the children. "Who did it?!" The little ones, Ella and Claude, start to cry. Adam, Helen, and Joan sit perched on the edge of their seats like deer in headlights.

"You little varmints!" He stands up, pulls off his belt, and raises it above their heads. Adam, Helen, and Joan slip off the bench and run up the stairs, the little ones following.

In the calmest manner possible I tell R.J. to put the belt down. He doesn't listen.

He brandishes the belt like a weapon, swinging it in the air, commanding the children to come back. They are terrified;

Claude and Ella start to wail. I plead with R.J. to stop, that they are just children, to please stop. I pull his shirt, he shrugs me off. The older three make it up the stairs to their bunk beds. Claude and Ella sit in the middle of the living room floor, mewling in each other's arms. He weilds the belt, ready to strike them. I rush in between him and the children. The hard leather strap stings my back. I don't care, I don't care, my babies, my babies. He doesn't stop until he tires out. He throws his belt down and slams the door as he leaves. My babies are shaking. "Shh, shh, it's okay." I carry them, one on each hip, up the stairs. I tuck them in their beds and check on the older ones. They are in their bunk beds, clinging onto their blankets. I kiss each of their foreheads and tell them it's going to be alright. I don't feel anything. I sit on the back porch, take in the night air.

I breathe in as crickets begin their evening song. Where can I go with five children? He can't do this again, must not do this again, never again. I want to cry. I can't. I want to fall. I can't.

He comes back late and enters through the porch door. I rush inside the kitchen. "Margaret," he whispers. I turn away. "Margaret, I'm sorry. I'm so sorry, I don't know what came over me. I just—" He tries to touch me. I dodge his hand.

"This can never happen again." I stack the children's plates and put them in the sink. Who is saying that? I am just a head without a body—where has my body gone?

"Margaret, Margaret, please . . ." My body gets up away from him and his contrition. I drift up the stairs, into our bedroom, and shut the door.

He sleeps on the couch that night and leaves early for work. The spilled milk and disarray of dishes clutter the kitchen table from the scene last night. I clear the rest of the plates, wipe the table and carefully rinse and dry the five silver cups and place them in the cupboard. Everything has its place. "Why, Margaret? Why do we have these silver cups?" he asked me the day we bought them. And I replied, "Because we can, R.J., because we can."

I get through the day, making breakfast for the children, cleaning up as the children play in the yard. I set the dinner table outside on the porch. It is warm enough, and maybe a change of scenery will help. He said he will bring home dinner. I am numb.

R.J. walks up the porch steps with flowers in one hand and Kentucky Fried Chicken in the other. He places the KFC on the table and hands me the bouquet. "I'm sorry, Margaret, I'm sorry." I take the flowers. "Margaret, aren't you going to say something? Anything?" He puts his hands in his pockets, shifting his feet.

"The children are hungry." I call them in for dinner. They scramble up the steps and burst through the porch door. They see him and freeze. It's as if they stop breathing all at once, waiting for a signal to exhale.

He displays the bucket of chicken. "Now who wants a drumstick?"

A chorus of voices clamors at once: "Me! Me! I want a drumstick!" The children sense his playfulness, that good Daddy is here now. They accept it as if he has always been this way. Ella and Claude raise their little hands and he drops a drumstick on each of their plates. They squeal with glee. Helen pouts, and he puts a drumstick on her plate; she takes it greedily. Joan and Adam wait patiently until he hands them the bucket. He catches my eye and quickly averts his gaze. "Come, Margaret, sit down." I take my seat across from him, gripping my coffee cup, watching every move.

The morning is my favorite time, before anyone awakes in the house, before the trill of the first bird. I roll out of bed, careful not to wake R.J. on the day he likes to sleep—Saturday. I gingerly walk down the steps and a baby wails. Is it Ella or Claude? It's Ella, she's standing at the side of her crib. I scoop her up quickly before Claude wakes up and walk down the stairs, past the kitchen and into the yard: my salvation. The dew on the grass seeps through my slippers. I press my hands in the cool soil, tears drop—the earth doesn't mind. Ella mimics me, her plump, brown fingers are tiny next to mine. The first light bathes the trees; the birds begin their morning songs. "Ella, it's the sun." She sits in my lap her cheek rests against mine. She points and says sun, sun. I sing her song to her, "Little Ella, Little Ella, she's the leader of the band, she can play the old piano, plink plink plink plink plank." This is Ella's song, all my children have them. She loves it at the end when I tickle her belly. I pull weeds from around the iris flowers that are beginning to bloom. Ella joins me. A ladybug lands on my hand. It visits a moment; I guide it to a stem and it gladly attaches itself. The coffee machine gurgles in the kitchen; R.J. must be awake. I know what I must do. I place Ella on my hip, walk into the kitchen, pick up the phone, and call the babysitter.

The farther north I drive, the more rugged rocks jut out from the shoreline, protecting sparse beaches below. Intermittently, lonely lighthouses appear set above the beach, desolate—as if waiting for a visitor. I head towards Munjoy Hill, in Portland. Memories flood me: playing in the street with Kenny, Sammy, and Hank, feet slapping on hard concrete, loud laughter. I pass the church where I lit a candle praying to the Virgin Mother, the church that denied my brother Lloyd a burial, little Lloyd. Divorce. Did I really dare? It is a sin against the church, the church that denied my poor brother. I recall the priest's words: "You'd make a good wife and mother." I don't want to disobey God, yet I don't know if I can stay with him. I'm at my mother's flat. It feels smaller now—and is more run down, paint chipping, steps a bit crooked, the steps I ran down as a little girl to get help from Aunt Jo. Maybe Aunt Jo is home. The lights aren't on in Aunt Jo's place; I better not disturb them. There in the yard stands my tree, sturdy in full bloom, preparing to drop acorns:

each acorn carrying the potential to seed a whole forest. As a child I relied on this tree: hiding with Hank from strange men and singing my heart out to it.

I knock on the door. My mother answers, surprised. "Margaret! What on earth—come in. Grandma Emma is here too!"

"Oh Mother!" And I start to sob, uncontrollably sob.

"Margaret, come sit. I'll make you a cup of tea." I sit down with my heavy head in my hands. I force myself to rise. Grandma Emma sits across from me with her back erect and lips drawn together. Her dark brown face is creased with lines. The kitchen table, green linoleum floor, and padded green chairs that used to stick to my legs as a child are all the same. Tears roll down my face; they won't stop now. My mother pours me a cup of tea. "I told you Margaret, there was something odd about him. I told you . . ."

"Yes, Mother, I know." I add milk and sugar into the cup, stirring it gently. "Most of the time it is good; he is a good, stable provider."

Emma observes me like an inquisitive bird. "Watch the children. You need to watch the children." She makes me nervous. My mother lights a cigarette.

"Mother, I thought you stopped?" I try not to sound too accusatory.

"Yes, I know, but this is a special occasion." She tilts her head as she blows the smoke to the side. "I can't give it all up, alcohol and cigarettes."

"Yes, I know, Mother."

"One day at a time, Margaret. So, what will you do?"

"I can't leave him. The children, where would we go? I can't make enough money nursing . . ."

"There, there, Margaret, chin up." Mother pats my back. "Just make the best of it, the best you can." She takes once last puff of her cigarette. The smoke irritates me. I open the window. "He's providing for you and your children, Margaret, that's a lot, a lot more than your father ever did." She grinds the end of the cigarette into the ashtray. Grandma Emma begins singing a song I don't recognize. She bangs the table. Her voice, guttural and percussive, snaps me out of my sadness—there is a fierceness to her words, an intention I don't understand.

"Emma does this now, sings in the old language, banging on the table like a drum." Mother places her hand on my shoulder. I hold onto it. We don't dare disrupt Emma's deep voice and clamor. She finishes her song, wraps her shawl around her shoulders, stands up, and leaves the room.

"Do you know what it means?" I ask my mother.

"No, but I do think she is praying for us—that is what I do believe."

PART III

ELLA

New York City, New York
1986

MOSTLY WHITE

It was my big sister Joan who taught me how to get back up no matter what. She took care of the neighbor's horses and she taught me how to ride. We'd ride through the trails and inevitably I'd get bucked off and crash down on my bottom in the dirt. Joan would tell me to get back on the horse and I'd cry and carry on, tell her it hurt, and she'd demand, "El, get back on the horse now!" And I'd get back on, sore bottom and all, and finish the trail ride. I'd forget about the fall until the next time. Nothing like riding through the woods. It was so freeing, and I felt as powerful as my big sister who knew how to tame the great horse beasts.

In the summer we ran barefoot. The first couple of days the soles of my feet were tender, and after a few days they hardened. All five of us, Joan, Adam, Helen, Claude, and I, would tear up the neighborhood. With our brown skin, wild hair, and bare feet, we waded in brooks across the street searching for crayfish and played endless games of pickle on soft grass. Claude and I always ended up in the middle. Kick the can, flashlight tag, ding-dong ditch it—those were the best times, when all five of us were free like a tribe until the sun went down.

We stayed outside as much as possible, away from our father and his unpredictable moods. My mom was busy getting her Master's; she was rarely home. He threw Claude once, clear across the yard. Claude was just a little boy, four years old. We were all outside and Dad was fixing a bike near the shed. Claude must have gotten in his way and he hurled him across the patch of garden. Claude cried and we all rushed to help him. We surrounded Dad. Adam was ready to strike him and I picked up a stick. Dad held the bicycle wheel in his hand. Adam confronted him. "Why'd you throw him?"

"Yeah, why, Dad?" Joan added. It was the first time I ever saw fear in his eyes. Now I was on the other side of fear; all of us together, we were formidable.

My dad held his hands up in the air, "I'm sorry, I won't do it again." He shuffled past us in his uneven gait, back to the house.

In the spring I ran in the woods before the mosquitos got bad. If I was quiet enough I'd see deer. I had a staring contest with one. It lasted a while. I was afraid of her and maybe she was afraid of me too. She leaped into the woods before I got too close to her. I never saw her again.

My secret place was the roof outside my window. At night I'd sit out there to sneak a cigarette and watch the stars. Nobody ever found out.

I had a big voice and I didn't know it until I got a part in the school play. I was the only one the audience could hear. After that, I decided I wanted to be an actress so I could take up all the space I wanted on stage and people would listen to me. My mother told me I could be anything I wanted, and I believed her. So here I am in New York City, here I am. The first thing I noticed about the city is that there are no stars in the sky. I know they're there, you just can't see them.

* * *

I feel ridiculous in this neon pink T-shirt with "Auntie Pasta" across my chest, black pants, and a black apron, well, at least I match the pink and green tablecloths covered with plastic surrounding me. The manager, Tom, hisses, "You need to go faster,

faster!" I call in an order to the kitchen, where they all speak Spanish; I rush to the bar to get table five's drinks. Keren, the other waitress on the floor, is Israeli. She looks like her name: elegant, cropped black bangs frame her heart-shaped face and full red lips. A beauty. I struggle to get my orders in, add up my checks correctly, serve customers the right food—

"Go faster!" Tom yells as I pass by.

Keren whispers, "Just ignore him." She walks cat-like to a new table to take their order.

There's a lull in the night and only a few tables remain. I'm exhausted: it's close to eleven p.m. I write on the back of the dessert list a snippet of a poem, feeling—

"What are you doing?" Tom roars at me. "You think you gonna be a writer? Famous? Hah!" He snatches the paper from my hand and throws it on the floor. "Get busy and clear your tables." My body stiffens; I can't move or breathe.

Keren passes by me and whispers, "Asshole," under her breath.

"What did you say?" Tom's face turns red.

Keren faces him. "I said you're an asshole."

Tom picks up a knife off the bar. "You called me what?" He points the knife at Keren.

As he lurches towards her, she screams, "Run!" We fly out the door, cold air hitting our faces.

We run down 6th Avenue. "You better run, you bitches, you better run, I'll kill you, I'll kill you!" Tom raises the knife in the air. Keren grabs my hand—we can no longer hear him and we run as if he's right behind us—until we reach 10th Street. We stop at the doorstep of the women's residency where I live, catching our breath.

Keren gets out a cigarette, hands me one. We smoke in silence. My hand starts to tremble; I can't stop shaking. I drop the cigarette.

"You okay?" Keren asks. I crouch on the stairs.

"He could have—he was coming right at you—us."

"Yeah, I know." Keren takes a sharp inhale of her cigarette. "Shit. I still have my apron on." I untie the black straps from my waist.

Keren takes the apron and holds it with her fist in the air. "A souvenir from the asshole!" And we bust out laughing so hard, I almost fall off the stairs.

"So, tell me, what is it that you want to do in New York?" she says curiously. I'm embarrassed to answer the most obvious answer, the most predictable—

"An actress, I want to be an actress like everyone else."

"Ah, an actress, of course! You know what I think you are?" She reminds me of a femme fatale from a film noir, the street light leaves her face half in shadow. She pauses dramatically, "You are an undiscovered princess."

"What?"

"An undiscovered princess, that's what you are." A princess? Where's my knight in shining armor? I laugh and take it as a compliment, coming from Keren. She puts her cigarette butt out on the step. "I'm meeting my boyfriend at Mars, you wanna come?"

"Mars?"

"Yes, you know the club Mars."

"Oh yeah, Mars." I don't know the club but I act like I do, just to appear cool. My nerves are shot, don't think I can handle a crowded place. I make up the excuse that I'm tired and Keren strolls down 10th street. I call after her, "Sorry we lost our jobs."

"Eh, there will be another one." Keren answers nonchalantly, I hope she's right.

That night I had a dream I was running in the woods, brown leaves on the ground. A boy behind me fell and I had to leave him there on the trail. I had to keep running. I was cold and dug in the ground for something to eat. I felt so bad that I left him on the trail, I kept moving . . . I woke up in a sweat.

Rent is due in a week. I need to find another job. I pick a

direction: uptown. Walking up 3rd Avenue, past 14th Street, 34th Street, 54th Street, I stop at a restaurant on 72nd. Jan's. The doors are open. A thin blond woman with straight hair and a sharp nose sits at the bar sizing me up.

"I'm wondering if you're hiring, are you the manager?"

"You have a resume?" I hand her mine, and she peruses it. "Well, we don't have any waiting jobs open but we could use another coat check girl." She points to a small closet. "Come in tonight at 6:30. The other girl will be here to train you."

"Okay, thanks." Mission accomplished.

Coat check girl—check your ego at the door. Oh, the glamour of New York. I sigh and fumble in my pockets for cigarettes—found a pack. Take one, light it; it's getting cold, even a little dark. The first inhale soothes me, the tobacco an offering to the sky. The smoke swirls above people's heads unnoticed—as unnoticeable as me. I'm at the corner of Bloomingdale's. No point in going in there, I have no money. I catch the 6 train downtown; got to get ready for my new job, new career.

At Jan's I meet the girl who's training me—beautiful, tall, long hair—must be a model. Her name is Lauren and her white teeth sparkle as she smiles at me. Lauren seems to have it together, looks and confidence, and to top it off she's kind. I immediately decide I'd like to be her, except I'm too short. On a good night we can make $100, not bad, and a bad night $30, still not too bad. Lauren shows me the closet and the numbered hooks and tickets for the customers. I need to memorize where each number is because the coats pile up in there.

She goes off talking to some guy she knows. I stand in this closet staring at the numbers underneath the hooks, trying to concentrate: 1 2 3 4 5 6 7 8 9 10 11 12 . . . here I am at another dead end job. Maybe I should have stayed in college, but I just want to be an actress. I'm barely making it now. I need to master these numbers, these hooks, so I can be a successful coat check girl! 23 24 25 26 27 28 29 . . .

Nancy, the red-faced, steel-blue-eyed manager, peeks her head in the closet. Lauren halts her conversation when Nancy motions her over.

"Is she getting the hang of it?"

"Yeah, she's a natural." Lauren nods towards me.

"Yeah," I answer. "I found my new calling." Nancy doesn't laugh. I guess she doesn't like jokes.

People come in: ladies with furs, guys with long woolen coats, leather jackets, nothing unsophisticated. Soon, the jackets pile up on top of each other and you cannot see any original hooks. Lauren points to the pile. "Now you understand why you need to know where the numbers are." She flirts effortlessly with the customers. A stylish older guy gives her a ticket, and she dives into the coats and disappears.

"Where did she go?" He winks at me.

"It's her magic trick." She comes out with his leather jacket.

"How did you do that?"

Lauren smiles. "I'm an expert." He steps towards her.

A woman comes up from behind him. "There you are, are you ready?" She purses her red lips. He shakes himself out of Lauren's beauty spell.

"Oh yes." He fumbles through his wallet and drops a twenty into the tip jar. It's Lauren magic.

My turn to dive into the coats and retrieve the right one. Customers are charmed by the pretty young coat check girls disappearing into layers of coats, emerging with static hair, proud smiles, and the correct garment. What a scene, what a treasure, look at all that New York can offer.

"Why are you so sad?" An older man approaches me, salt and pepper curly hair, blue eyes. "You're much too beautiful to be so sad."

I try to smile. "Gotta ticket?" He places his ticket into my hand. I expertly dive into the coats feeling for number 23. Got it. I pull it out.

"Aren't you something!"

"I'm a professional."

"I can see that. What are you really? An actress?"

"Isn't everybody?"

"You have a look. I'm an agent, here's my card. You should give me a call."

"Thanks." I take the card.

"I'm Bruce." We shake hands.

"Ella." He puts his other hand on top of mine.

"Be sure to call me, Ella." He releases his hand slowly, and winks at me before he leaves.

Lauren comes back from the bar. "Almost over."

"Yeah," I say. She dumps over the tip jar and begins counting. We had a good night.

It's one o'clock by the time my shift is over. Nancy, red-faced and angry, chastises a waitress at the end of the bar. I say goodbye to Lauren, who is talking up some guy in a suit at the bar. I put on my coat and open the door; cold night air hits my face. I reach into my pocket. The card, oh yeah, the card. I think of hope.

The rent line is long at the Katherine House Women's Residency. Girls ahead of me clutch check books and shift their weight. The air is stuffy, tight, like you're not supposed to breathe. The drama queen stands in front of me, silky light brown hair, porcelain skin. She always scowls at me. She takes up the phone in the hall; I can hear her yelling at her boyfriend with my door closed. Her nickname: "DQ." The owner of the Katherine House sits regally at her desk. She wears her hair piled up on top of her head in curls. There are rules in her house, the number one being no male guests in your rooms at night. A picture of Jesus hangs to the right of her desk, reminding us this place is owned by Catholics and Jesus is watching us.

To kill time, I leave the line to play the piano in the living room. It's a bit out of tune, and every so often when no one is there I sing and play. I lose myself in some music, then get back in line—it's much shorter now. The landlady takes my check. "Was that you playing the piano?"

"Yes."

"Well, you are not allowed to play it after nine." She speaks in an authoritative clipped tone, like a school teacher. She writes a receipt in perfect cursive. Relieved I paid rent, though my room with its linoleum floor reminds me of a hospital, and I know someone stole my bike I had in storage downstairs—Jesus, are you watching? I rush to the phone in the hall only to find DQ in the phone booth—it's the make-up call—better than the breakup call with all the yelling and crying.

"I know, I miss you too . . . what am I wearing? Stop!" She giggles into the phone and shoots me one of her perfect scowls. I wait with folded arms. Finally, she gets off the phone—kissing her goodbyes—and walks out, tossing her silky hair behind her. I dial Bruce's number.

"Stage Door Talent, can I help you?" She has a distinct nasal tone to her voice.

"Yes, I'd like to speak to Bruce please." I articulate my words as much as possible to sound professional.

"May I ask who's calling?"

"Ella, the coat check girl." Why did I say that? There's a pause and muffled sounds. My heart pounds in my chest, he remembers me. Phew! We make an afternoon appointment. I scribble down the address on a corner of the telephone book, 459 33rd Street, thank him and hang up the phone. This could be my big chance, my big break, my—I suck in my gut feeling a little fat, decide to go with a tank top, big sweater, and jeans.

I catch the R train and get off at 36th street. I feel like throwing up—lightheaded, not real. I feel pretty enough, I think.

I take the elevator up to the 7th floor, to Stage Door Talent. The office is small and cramped. A man yells on the phone in the back room: "I tell you I will never let my daughter be an actress, never, no way. This shit is—" he shuts the door.

The receptionist, a mousy girl with glasses, plays it off like we hadn't heard a thing. "May I help you?" She has a nasal sound when speaking on the phone and in person.

"Yes." I manage to speak. "I'm here to see Bruce."

"Oh yes, just a minute." She picks up the phone, the yelling stops. My hands sweat and Bruce swings in, all smiles.

"Great you made it, come on in. Meet my partner Andy."

Andy grimaces while on the phone. "Where'd you find her?"

"Underneath a pile of coats." Bruce winks at me.

Andy's expression doesn't change. "Take off your sweater."

"Huh?"

"It's okay," Bruce reassures me. "He just wants to know what parts you'd be good for."

They both wait. I take off my big sweater. Andy says, "Turn around." I turn around. "You need to lose five pounds, but you've got something exotic." Andy scans up and down my body.

"You know, she'd be good for that Coca-Cola spot." He and Bruce exchange silent approval. I suck in my gut.

"Oh yeah, I'll take care of it," Bruce responds.

Bruce puts his arm around me and guides me towards the door. I put my sweater back on. "I need to take some shots of you at the studio. Let's catch a cab uptown." My stomach feels queasy—just nerves? We take the elevator down and I'm glad to get out of there, away from "take off your sweater" guy. Bruce hails a cab and we're off.

"So, you need photos? I have an eight-by-ten here." I start taking it out of my bag.

"It's standard," Bruce answers. "We need to get as many shots as possible to get you out there. You are beautiful, you know that?" He strokes my hand. "A young Natalie Wood." We get out of the cab at his building, pass his doorman and take the elevator to the 11th floor.

"This is your studio?" I ask nervously.

"Yes, I live here too." My heart races. He turns the key in the door. White plush carpeting, a view from the window, city lights—

"Where's the studio?"

"Just relax, sweetheart, I'm not going to bite." He flops his briefcase and coat down on the couch. "You want a drink? I'm going to make a drink."

"No, thanks."

Ice clinks against his glass as he takes a sip. "Ahhhh. Okay, come this way." He takes my hand and leads me through a short hallway into a room with wood floors, a black umbrella and lights in front of a backdrop.

"Here it is. Take off your sweater." I take it off, stand in front of him, he flashes the camera over and over. "Lift your chin—smile now—okay, like you want something—show me desire—oh honey, beautiful." I feel hot with lights on me. I feel like a star.

"What are you, Puerto Rican?"

"No, I'm mixed. Well, white, Native American, and a little black . . ."

"Oooh, how exotic, a hybrid. Hybrids are the most beautiful flowers, you know." The camera flashes stop and he caresses my face. I am a flower in a glass case—trapped. "You're a real natural, you know." He slides his hand down my neck, down my shirt, over my breasts. I don't stop him—I am frozen, a frozen exotic flower, a natural, a star, he unzips my jeans, takes off my shirt, bra—

"Oh honey, you are so hot, let me take you." He thrusts himself into me, pinning me down. "Come on, baby, come on." I am still a flower, I am still exotic.

"Are you hungry?" He puts his pants on, I pull my shirt to my chest. He leaves me on the floor. I put my clothes on. Wow, so this is "standard." I walk into the living room, and he's lying on the couch.

"Baby, I'm beat. You don't mind making me a sandwich."

"No, that's fine." I don't know who's talking, who's speaking. He lights a cigarette, and I go into the kitchen, open the fridge and make him a tuna fish sandwich. I place it on the coffee table. He scrutinizes me. "You're one of the givers, aren't you?"

"What?"

"Givers, you're a giver like Jesus Christ."

"Huh, I don't know." What does the picture of Jesus hanging in the landlady's office have to do with me? I don't get the connection. I take a cigarette out of my bag and light it.

"You know, you have a Coke commercial tomorrow."

I inhale, my head feels light. I exhale. "Okay."

Bruce walks me to the elevator, kisses me on the forehead and embraces me. "Oh, my little Natalie Wood." The elevator door closes, his hands search all over my body. "My exotic flower." The door opens, he takes my hand, the doorman nods at him—where am I? Bruce hails a cab, whispers into my ear, "Come to my place after the Coke audition. Good luck." He pats me on my butt, I get in the cab. The cab driver asks me "Where to?"

"One eighteen west Thirteenth Street." My voice feels far away from my body. I can't feel my arms or my legs: it's like they belong to somebody else.

Hot shower hot shower hot shower, middle of the day, no one else there. I rock back and forth in the hot water and steam. What's happening to me? I'm a good girl, grew up in the suburbs, had piano lessons, went to college—well, for a while. I start to crack, break—got to pull it together for work, for diving into coats tonight.

* * *

My audition is at 12:30. I'm five minutes early. I hand the receptionist my headshot. She gestures me to a chair. I try and feel something. All those acting classes: Meisner, Strasberg,

Chekhov—here's my moment: Coca-Cola.

Two handsome, dark-haired men greet me and tell me to go into a room for a screening. I take off my coat and enter the room. It's sealed off, I am in a box—they can see me but I can't see them. I can only hear them. "Okay, so we're going to play some music and as soon as you hear the music, dance."

Weird for a Coke commercial. Fast-paced music blares. I can't make it out, it's not in English but Spanish. The only word I catch is "Coca-Cola." They yell at me, "Dance! Dance! Dance!"

I jump up and down a little, sway my hips. The music stops. I freeze. Silence. Hmmm. Not a good sign. A voice: "Okay, that's it, you can go."

I get my coat and leave. No one says goodbye. I walk out of the building and sunlight bounces off cars. I head uptown. I don't feel my feet on the ground—like I am hovering above myself. Woah, what was that? I jump back as a hummingbird flutters in front of me and flies off. A hummingbird on 3rd Avenue? For a moment I feel possibilities, beauty in this concrete world.

My body takes me to Bruce's apartment, like he told me to do. The doorman lets me in. I take the elevator up to Bruce's place. I knock, he opens the door.

"How'd it go?"

I cry. I just cry and I let him embrace me. "Why didn't you tell me it was in Spanish?"

"Well, we wouldn't send you to a regular commercial—they want the girl next door, white girls."

I can't believe he's saying this. I am the girl next door—aren't I? Mostly—

"Check out these photos, baby." He picks up glossy black and white eight-by-tens from the counter and hands them to me.

My face is white enough—isn't it? Well, compared to Drama Queen with her silky hair and porcelain skin—nah. So, who is that Hawaiian girl in that photo? And it hits me. It hits me like it never has before: I AM NOT WHITE.

Bruce leads me to the couch. "Come on, baby, come here." He opens his arms, and I know my body will follow him, know it. I sit on his lap.

"I want to be a real actress . . ."

"Of course you do, baby, you could do the soaps—with that face." His fingers gently trace my cheeks, chin, down my neck, down my shirt. I let him. He takes my hand, leads me to his bedroom. I am nobody.

"Now let me see you." He brushes my hair back with his hand, kisses my mouth, my hands are around his neck pulling his hair. He unbuttons my blouse, takes off my bra, cups my breasts in his hands, kissing them—he unzips my jeans and places me on the bed. "Let me see you." His hands run up and down my body. I am some body, I am his. All that is going through my head is that music from the Coke commercial.

I wake up in the middle of the night, "Dance! Dance! Dance!" blaring in my head—where am I? Bruce snores. I find my underwear, crawl under the covers to get my bra, blouse, jeans and put myself back together. What am I doing? Tuna fish sandwiches, Natalie Wood, exotic flower, let me see you let me see you I'd never let my daughter be an actress take off your sweater turn around you'd never get cast for the girl next door ooh baby does it feel good does it? Dance! Dance! Dance!

I want to shut off my brain. I examine my face in the bathroom mirror and remind myself: I'm not white. Creeping out of Bruce's apartment, I can't help myself. I make him a tuna fish sandwich. Yeah, I guess he's right—I am a giver.

INXS blares in my ears as I jog around Washington Park with my Walkman. Around and around the park, the only place downtown to jog and not have to stop for traffic. I don't mind the circles, breathing in, breathing out, trying to shake off last night—the surrender of myself to that man and that ridiculous audition. Who am I? Oh yeah, apparently not white . . .

enough—breathing in breathing out, I swerve in between students, lovers holding hands, people walking with direction, fortitude, like their steps belong to the earth. Where's my ground? Where's my ground?

I thought I was white, growing up in New England. I asked my mom in the car driving me home from a friend's house. "What am I, Mom?"

"What do you mean?" My mother responded in her soft-spoken way.

"What race? Am I black, white, Indian? People ask me, I don't know what to say." She paused for a long time.

"Well, you are mostly white."

"White?"

"Yes, Irish . . . mostly white."

I accepted her answer although it confused me. I didn't fit into this version of myself. I put clothespins on my nose overnight because I thought it would make it thinner. No one at school looked like me. I needed to look like them. They were the beautiful people in movies and on TV. They were like Dad.

I only met his relatives once, in Arkansas. All seven of us flew in an airplane down south. Mom bought me a new dress and red and white canvas pump sandals to match. We all got something new to wear to meet our relatives. I was excited to wear my new outfit on the plane. I hoped they liked us.

The sky was bright blue, the air thick and hot when we got off the plane. We rented a car and drove a long way, passing wooden shacks every so often with black people staring back at us with resentful eyes. Nobody said anything in the car. We just passed by, all five of us children curious about this new land, Arkansas. I spotted a dead carcass on the road.

"What was that?" I asked Dad.

"Oh, probably an armadillo, we have lots of them here. We are almost at the ranch, Uncle Ray's—your great uncle, my father's brother—and Elsie's, his wife. My mother will be there, your grandmother Maribelle, and my father Edward. Very nice people, children, so be on your best behavior, you all understand?" We responded in silence. I couldn't keep all those names straight in my head.

Our red rent-a-car sedan turned into a long dirt driveway, flat land, the trees tired and heavy from the heat. We stopped at a white modern house that reminded me of the Brady Bunch house, on sprawling land.

"I have to go to the bathroom!" Claude whined, as he wiggled in his seat.

"You'll have to wait till we get inside," my father snapped back.

"Honey, just get out of the car and you can go inside, okay?" My mother calmed him with her voice. The hot air assaulted us as we piled out of the car. My father rang the doorbell. My mother held onto Claude's hand. A big burly white man with balding gray hair answered the door.

"Why R.J., come on in, so glad you made it!" He patted Dad's back.

"Uncle Ray, thank you for the invitation." They shook hands, grinning at each other.

"Come on now, come in and get out of the heat. We have air conditioning on." Great Uncle Ray gestured at us to come inside. The house was comfortable, an open kitchen and living room. Sliding glass doors led to the outside, a fenced-in pasture. Joan, the eldest, Adam, Helen, me, and Claude walked cautiously into the living room. Mom rushed Claude to the bathroom.

"Well, these must be R.J.'s children!" An older woman in glasses got up off a lazy chair to greet us.

"Yes, Aunt Elsie, these are my children. Joan, Adam, Helen, Ella, and Claude, the little one, is in the bathroom with Margaret."

"Well, y'all must be thirsty after that long drive, would y'all like some lemonade?" We nodded our heads politely. "Come into the kitchen now. I'll pour you a glass."

"That's mighty kind of you, Elsie, mighty kind," my father replied for us. We followed our Great Aunt Elsie into the kitchen.

"Now, if you children want to go outside and meet our cows, they are right there beyond the glass door." The doorbell rang. Great Uncle Ray answered it.

"There you two are! R.J. and his crew just came in. R.J., your parents are here."

My father greeted his parents. "Mama, Papa. Come on in."

"Now, I don't have to be invited into my brother's house, I come in here all the time." A tall, bald, white man holding a hat walked briskly past my father.

"Oh don't mind him, R.J. Oh my, you are getting old, aren't you?" An older woman embraced my dad.

"Mama, we all are, we all are. Come meet Margaret and the children." She was friendlier than her husband, her hair snow white with a tint of blue, styled in curls.

"Why, you must be Margaret?" She held her hand out to my mother, who had come out of the bathroom with Claude.

"Yes, and you must be Maribelle." My mother smiled graciously and took her hand.

"I'm so glad you and Papa came out today," my father interjected. "Come meet the rest." As we sipped our lemonade in the kitchen, the tall, angry bald man talked with Uncle Ray in the living room. I could tell they were having a heated discussion.

"Come on, you all, come meet your Grandma Maribelle, my mother."

We crowded around her and she said, "Jesus loves you, every one of you very much. Know that, he loves you so much!" She had tears in her light blue eyes as she spoke. We all just shrugged our shoulders and tried to smile and be polite.

"Maribelle, come get some lemonade, sure is hot enough. There is a pool for you children, but that's where them niggers swim, it's awful. I wouldn't go in that pool." Elsie handed Grandma Maribelle a glass of lemonade.

Uncle Ray came over with his empty glass, "Them niggers are everywhere now, can't get rid of them." He filled up his glass. My mother's face hardened. She stood clasping her glass of lemonade so I hard I thought it was gonna break. I waited for her to say something, to tell them to stop. She didn't say a word. My father coughed nervously.

The angry bald man, Grandpa Edward, joined in. "They don't know their place anymore. These niggers think they can do what they want now. Just anything they want." He gulped down his lemonade and stepped in front of my father to pour himself another glass. I'm confused. Don't they know we are part black? Don't they know my mother is part black? Why are they talking like this? Why doesn't Mom or Dad say anything?

"Edward, come meet your grandchildren," Maribelle cut in, her voice shaking.

The angry bald man grimaced at us, his knuckles white from gripping his hat as if he were going to rip it. "These are a bunch of bastards, that's what they are."

All five of us, without saying a word, headed for the sliding glass doors. Outside, the stench of cow dung immediately hit our noses, we didn't care. The cows, stoic and silent, stood in the mud and manure, pacified by the intense heat of the sun. "It's not right, this mixing is not right. Those children are not my kin, I tell you they are bastards!" It was Grandpa Edward's voice. "A bunch of nigger children you have brought here—it's not natural."

"That's enough, Edward, they are your grandchildren!" Grandma Maribelle reprimanded him. A door slammed. I stepped farther out in the pasture. My red and white sandals sunk deep in the muck and my brothers and sisters petted the cows, waiting until it was time to go.

It is my last time around the park. I want to believe desperately, believe in something. Yes, I am an actress, I am—

Breathe in, breathe out.

I run back down 5th Avenue and take a left on 13th Street to the Katherine House, I keep going. Rage fills my chest as my feet pound the pavement all the way down 13th Street to the Hudson River. At the edge of the pier seagulls dip in and out of clouds. I hunch over, trying to catch my breath. The seagulls caw above. Something shiny and gray comes to the surface—a dead body? I move closer and a creature leaps out of the water in front of me. I stumble and almost fall in the river. Was it a dolphin or maybe a porpoise? I search the water. Nothing's there, but I know I saw something. I brush it off and jog back to the Katherine House to jump in the shower before taking the 6 train uptown.

At Jan's restaurant, Nancy is at the bar, flipping pages of a magazine. She barely acknowledges me. "Oh, we only need one coat check girl now." I stop in my tracks.

"Why?"

"Spring, less jackets." She lights a cigarette.

"Well fuck you then!" I say, and turn around before she can say anything back, greeting the uncertainty of the outside air. Okay, I won't use her for a referral. Something will work out, just pick a direction. This time I decide south. I take the 6 train back downtown and get off at Astor Place.

I drop off my resume at a few places, no luck. I'm almost in Soho when I spot a sign: "Fine Italian Cuisine." Maybe they're hiring. It's a fancy place with a piano in front of dining tables. I ask a stocky man with curly brown hair if they are hiring. He sizes me up from head to toe. "You sing?"

"Yes, I do."

"Good, 'cause we need waitresses that sing." He checks out my body once more. I squeeze in my stomach and hand him my resume. "Good, good. I'm Joey, one of the managers here." He offers his hand and sniffs. His eyes shift as he speaks. Hmm, I wonder, cocaine?

"I'm Ella." I shake his hand. He abruptly lets his hand go.

"Let's find Tony." He walks fast, I can barely keep up. We enter an office. "Tony, we need a new waitress?"

Tony shuffles his papers. "Yeah, Joey, who's this?" Tony is identical to Joey; I can only tell them apart because Joey wears a tie.

"I'm Ella." I offer my hand, he doesn't take it.

"She'll do. Show her around." He goes back to his papers.

"This way." Joey motions me. He takes me to the staff room, a narrow hall with gray lockers and a time card punch. "This is where you'll punch in. You can start training tonight trailing Michael, our head waiter." I follow him out to the dining room. He stops at the piano. "Let's hear you sing." He folds his arms in front of him. "Don't be shy, sweetheart, the mic is right here."

"Oh, okay, um, I'll play the piano."

"Whatever you want."

I sit down and start playing "I'm Wishing on a Star." I let the music take me, throwing sound into space. Joey places his hand on my shoulder. I stop singing, and he whispers, "You make me hard."

"Does that mean I get the job?" Another replica of Tony walks towards us. I know it's not Tony because this man has a blue shirt on, not white.

"Ah, Vinnie, meet Ella, our new waitress." He offers me his hand, and I take it. I smile nervously; he doesn't smile back.

Joey touches my back. "Here, let me walk you out." Joey leads me to the door, "Wear black and whites tonight and be here at five sharp." He opens the door. "See you tonight, beautiful." His hand trails down my back, gliding over my bottom as I walk out.

Okay, I get it—triplets. Vinnie, Tony, and Joey. Joey, what am I going to do about that one? I'll just try and stay away from him. Only problem is I won't know which one he is. At least I have a job now. I walk, singing all the way home.

Michael, the head waiter, is tall, with black hair, long delicate fingers, and crooked teeth. He's a musician. "Make sure you put the salad fork here. If you make a mistake, watch out for Vinnie. Vinnie will have a fit." He places the silverware down gently with precision. He's patient with me as I memorize the proper settings for the salad forks, dinner forks, knives, spoons, water glasses, and wine glasses. I follow him with a stack of bread plates; a triplet appears out of nowhere,

"How's she doing?" his nose is red and his head darts from side to side as he talks.

"Oh fine, fine, she's a quick learner." Michael smiles.

"Good, I'm expecting a lot out of you." He winks at me. Joey? Or Vinnie? I have no idea.

I trail Michael the whole night, studying his every move, until one of the triplets tells me to meet him in the office to finish some paperwork. They all wear the same white shirt, blue tie, and gray blazer. I wasn't sure who it was. I enter the office, he sits on a desk holding a folder.

"How's it going?" He gets up and closes the door behind me.

"Fine, you said there was some paperwork?" Why did he close the door?

"Yes, just forms, on the desk." He points to the papers, I walk to the desk to pick up the forms. He blocks my hand, holds my wrists up, and yanks me to him.

"Come on, aren't you turned on?" I try to push him away.

"I just came here for some paperwork." I shove him, and rush to the door.

"You're a fucking tease!" He slams his fists down on the desk. I can guess that one is Joey.

I try to collect myself and head to the staff lockers. Michael stops me. "There you are. Where'd you disappear to?"

"Oh, ah, paperwork, filling out, you know, papers . . ." I

open my locker and get my leather coat. Michael jingles his car keys and offers me a ride home. I need air, I need to feel my feet on the ground, even though it's, late I don't care. I need to walk, I need to get away from all these men, groping at me.

"Ah, no, no, I like to walk." I answer as we punch out our time cards, and head outside.

"Sure you don't need a ride?" No don't cry, don't cry Ella. "You okay?" Michael touches my shoulder. I flinch.

"Yeah, I'm fine, just a long day, so see you tomorrow." Michael lingers a while, waiting for me to change my mind. He gets the hint and continues down the street.

A barrage of men run through my head: Bruce with his quick hands and false promises, Joey and his rough touch. Why can't I stop these men? I need this job, I'm just going to make it work—what the hell am I doing? Michael is sweet. How gently he placed silverware on the table, how kind he was to me, I can't stop crying.

I wait at the curb for the light to change, tell myself, "Get ahold of yourself, Ella!" I walk to the nearest deli and buy the latest *Backstage*. I spot an open audition, a cattle call for a movie: *"Looking for young ethnic girls for the lead role, B movie."* I rip out the section and put it in my back pocket.

My first night waiting tables at my new job, at every turn Joey, Vinnie, or Tony barks orders at me, yet I never know who, I can't keep them straight—

"Make sure you comp table ten's drink, tell them it's on me!"

"Excuse me, you are . . . ?" And he zips away before I can find out.

Another triplet rushes past me. "Keep up the pace, you just got a new table!"

I quickly attend to them. I hurry to the kitchen, ring the bell, and tell them to fire table eight. The cooks are sweating and stressed; it's a busy night. I'm in the weeds with a full section.

A triplet stops me.

"Go to table ten, they've been waiting." I take their order and another table's drink order.

Another triplet accosts me. "How's it going? Did you push the specials? We need to push our lasagna tonight, got it? Push!" He brushes past me and I forget what drinks my new table ordered.

I approach the elderly white couple. The husband has a frown on his face, and the wife holds her head erect so as not to topple the red hair piled on her head—a wig? "Excuse me, sir, could you please repeat your drink order for me?"

"Hmmmm, what?"

"I'm sorry, could you please repeat your drink order for me? I seem to have forgotten."

"Aren't you a professional?"

"Yes, well, this is my first night here."

"Come on, Alan, don't be cruel, just tell her!" his wife pipes in with a thick New York accent. He reluctantly complies.

"A gin and tonic for the lady and a vodka martini for me. Can you remember that?" He sneers at me.

"Oh yes, sir, so sorry." I hurry to the bar, pick up their drinks, and take their dinner order. I want to smash something. I want to pick up a plate and smash it to the ground—time to clear table seven and take the dessert order. In the corner of my eye I spot the elderly couple conversing with one of the triplets and gesturing towards me. Uh oh. I quickly engage in conversation with customers, write down their dessert order, and attempt to circumvent a triplet on the way to the bar, too late. He stops me abruptly like a bull.

"They tell me you forgot their drink order. That table is a regular here, you understand? We don't allow mistakes here!" Veins pop out on the sides of his neck. Vinnie? Tony? He grips my arm, pulling me to the hallway. "You better be careful, because I've got my eyes on you." I break away. Joey, that was Joey.

I push my tears down. Michael stops me. "You okay? Joey really gave it to you." He gently touches my back. "Brush it off, he does it to everyone."

"I bet he does," I say inaudibly. Joey barrels through Michael and me.

"There's no time for flirting, get to your stations!" We hurry to the dining room like obedient children. Damn! I forgot to drop the order for table ten, the drink mishap table. Oh boy. I ring the kitchen bell; the cook wipes his brow and takes the ticket.

There is a lull in the restaurant, a rarity: you can feel your feet on the ground. One of the waitstaff takes this opportunity to sing. She cues the piano player and performs a Broadway tune; the crowd loves it. She beams at the applause and the pianist takes the mic. "Anyone else want to sing?"

One of the staff suggests, "What about the new girl?"

The waitstaff urges me on and I feel my face redden. Michael nods at me. I sit at the piano and play the introduction to "The Greatest Love of All." All the rage, pain, and sadness I feel in the pit of my stomach pushes out in sound. I can't stop it, as if I am a volcano and have no choice but to erupt at this moment—

I can't finish the song. I start crying at the piano. A man clears his throat. Michael touches my back and guides me out of the dining room into the staff room. I'm still sobbing, this volcano of grief outpours. Michael asks another waiter to cover his tables, helps me put my coat on, and leads me out the door.

"Wait, I forgot to fire table ten!" I start laughing and crying. "I guess the triplets won't want me back." I try to compose myself, take out a cigarette. Michael lights it.

"You okay?" He has kind brown eyes, and he's tall—I have to tilt my neck up to talk to him.

"Every once in a while, I need to have a public breakdown." I laugh.

"Come on, I'll take you home." Home, home—where the

hell is home? A tiny room with a linoleum floor, bed, and dresser, home? The shouts of the DQ on the phone in the hallway, the stale smell of the living room, the "no men allowed in your rooms" rule? No, I don't want to go home.

"I can't go there . . . not now."

Michael takes my arm. "Okay, how do you feel about Queens?" I shrug my shoulders, take the last drag of my cigarette, flick it on the sidewalk, and squash it with my heel. Queens sounds fine. We head for the subway. Michael has his arm around me like I'm some fragile thing that will break again if not careful. We walk up the subway steps into Queens. It's quieter than the city, fewer people on the street. "Let's go in here for a drink." As Michael opens the door for me, a bell rings. It's a dive: a few people sit at the bar nursing drinks, a stone-faced bartender cleans a glass and nods at us. We sit down; Michael orders tequila shots. We drink, a lot. I feel delirious. Michael kisses me—he tells me he loves me. I believe him. Every so often I catch scorn on the bartender's face, nearly imperceptible but there, as if he's witnessed thousands of couples like Michael and me. Maybe it's boredom. After the fourth shot Michael embraces me. "Let's get married." My drunken stupor matches his and I agree. We wobble out together, Michael shouting, "We're getting married!" The bartender doesn't change his expression. His dull eyes follow us as we leave.

We walk up to his flat; he carries me into his bedroom and flops me on his bed. I laugh, we kiss, he unbuttons my shirt, unhooks my bra, shoves his tongue in my mouth. "You're beautiful, you know that?" His long fingers run over my body. He unwraps a condom and swears as he comes. Maybe he should have at least said my name.

It's morning. I don't know where I am—and I half remember something about getting married. I crawl out from underneath Michael's arms; he's passed out. Here I go trying to find my underwear again in some man's bed. Shit! When will things change? My head feels like a knife is going through it—shit, shit, what am I doing here? Digging under the covers, I find them. Careful not to wake him, I dress and use the bathroom.

I whisper to Michael and tell him I have to go, he pulls my arms and kisses me, trying to get me in bed again. "I can't stay, I got an audition." He reluctantly releases me.

"Ella, call me later?" He says it like a question, he must sense I'm not going to.

"Okay." I walk out the door, down the steps, head throbbing, spot the subway and take the R train back downtown.

NOSE HAIR

I throw off my clothes and jump in the shower. I have forty-five minutes to get to the audition. I decide on a black mini skirt and a bright green t-shirt with pumps—casual, sexy. My hair is good enough. I head out the door, take the subway uptown, and fumble for the address in my pocket. Get off uptown—ouch, my head still hurts a little. I feel dull from the tequila last night. It's a place on Broadway, an older building. I enter a room full of long-haired beauties. I'm not late. A man with a clipboard assesses everyone in the room, whispering to a woman in a pantsuit, pointing discreetly at our bodies. "Okay," the man with the clipboard says authoritatively. "If I point to you, go to the front." He ponders a minute and points his finger. "You, you, you—" and he pauses and points to me. "You."

My face flushes. "Really, me?" I join the line of the lucky girls, about ten of us, all legs and long brown hair.

"The rest of you can go." Sighs permeate the room and the unlucky girls tread out with heavy limbs and rounded shoulders. We, the triumphant, wait for our cue from the important, clipboard-wielding man. "All right, we will meet you one at a time. Form a line here." We shuffle into a line; the energy thickens between us. We're the chosen, but only one can be the star of—

Wait, what movie is this? Well, whatever, there can only be one star. It's my turn. I shake hands with the clipboard man and smile.

"Name please." He doesn't smile back.

"Ella."

"Stand on this mark, and get your photo taken." I walk to the X taped on the floor, stand on it, and pose as the photographer takes the Polaroid.

"Come back tomorrow at four for your screening. Here's the address." He hands me a sheet of paper and motions a girl to come forward. "Next."

They chose me. A callback from a cattle call, a rarity. I grasp the paper in my hand as I descend the subway stairs.

It is a cheap hotel room, everything beige and gray. I check in with the receptionist, the same woman from the cattle call, and she hands me the scene. I sit in a chair facing the door with the other anxious girls, and begin studying the script:

(ANGELINA and FREDDIE are in bed, FREDDIE is on top of her. Camera closeup of ANGELINA's chest. Cut away to door opening. A man in a black hat enters with gun, points it at FREDDIE. FREDDIE reaches for his gun on the dresser, the man shoots him in the head. ANGELINA screams. Camera pans to closeup of brain splatter on shoe.)

SCENE II: The Confession

(ANGELINA walks into church and enters the confessional. Camera closeup of her face.)

ANGELINA—Forgive me, Father, for I have sinned.

PRIEST—How long has it been since your last confession, my child?

ANGELINA—Father, I, I—(She starts to cry.)

PRIEST—What is it, my child?

ANGELINA—Father, forgive me, Father—(Crying.)

PRIEST—Yes, child, yes, what is it?

ANGELINA—I have been sleeping with a married man and, and, (Sobs.) he was shot, killed, we were in bed and he was shot!

PRIEST—(Wipes his brow.) My child! This is very grave indeed!

ANGELINA—I loved him!!! And we were punished by God because we committed a sin and now he's gone, he's gone . . . murdered!

PRIEST—(Wipes brow again.) Child, this may not be because of your actions. He may have been shot because of something he did. You could be in danger, my child. Who is this man? Did the shooter see you?

ANGELINA—Yes, I'm sure of it. The shooter saw me. He was my love, my love, Antonio, he owns the bar on the corner. Antonio, my love!

PRIEST—(Shocked.) You are in grave danger, my child, grave danger . . . (Cut to ANGELINA sobbing, fade out.)

Who wrote this crap? "Brain splatter on shoe." High art. This is what you have to do as an actress—get exposure. Can't start at the top, or with your clothes on, right? B movie, okay, okay, how am I going to get into this character?

They call my name. I stand up and enter a small room, white walls and a plush gray carpet. A tall, older white man smiles at me, and a black woman with dreads introduces herself as the director and the man as Mike, who will play the priest.

The cameraman stands by his equipment with coffee cup in hand. His blond hair sticks up in the front—gel, probably. He smiles at me. I turn the other way. The priest actor puts his hand on my shoulder and makes eye contact.

"Ella, I just want you to know I'm going to be right here for you, even though in the scene we can't see each other," he says fervently like a serious actor. Meisner method, I think.

The director motions me over to my mark.

"Ella, enter here, sit there, remember you don't really see

the priest since you are in a confessional. Take your time." She signals the cameraman. He nods. I stand on my mark trying to memorize the first line. The director focuses on me intently. I search for something sad to take me into this character, and all that comes up is the cutaway to brain splatter on the shoe, and I want to laugh. The priest leans back in his chair. I dive in.

"Forgive me, Father, for I have sinned."

Halfway through the scene the director yells, "Cut!" I stop. I blew it. The priest runs his fingers through his hair. The cute blond cameraman stands up and takes a sip of coffee. The director takes me aside. "Nice, but we need tears, okay? Try again." I diligently go back to my spot; the priest readjusts his seat. Okay, pressure—tears on demand. I got nothing. I step off my mark, begin again. No tears. We do two more takes, still I'm not crying. The director takes me aside once more. "We really want you for this role. All we need are tears, so why don't you take a break, and we'll try again. Do what you need to do."

The priest chimes in, "I know it's hard to find the right way."

"Yeah, uh, is there a bathroom?"

"Sure, the door on the left."

"Thanks." I'm embarrassed I can't find tears. What kind of actress am I? I open the door to the bathroom. The sink is solid porcelain with a stain down the middle, the mirror has a crack on the side. I give myself a pep talk. "Come on, Ella, come on." Maybe I should put water on my eyes for fake tears, but would Meryl Streep do that? The sex scene, the brain splatter: she would never be asked to do any of this. And I don't care. I don't care about this film or this poorly written script—not enough to cry, anyways. I open the door and the director smiles.

"Ready?"

"I'm sorry but this isn't for me."

Her mouth gapes open in amazement; the priest clears his throat.

She tries to reassure me. "Come on, you are really great for this role."

"It's just not for me."

"You couldn't get to tears, why don't you try what he does?" She points to the priest.

"What do you do?" I ask him.

"I pull out a nose hair," he says proudly.

"Oh no, no. I'm not doing that." I hand the director the script. She is speechless.

"Okay, everybody take five." She drops the script on the table.

I walk out the door, glad to get out of the room, and sigh loudly in the lobby.

"That was quite an exit." I turn around—it's the blond cameraman. I push the down button for the elevator. "You got class." He smells like fresh soap and hair gel.

"Why, 'cause I won't pull out a nose hair?"

"Obviously that script sucks."

"Yes, yes, it really does." I like his wide shoulders, leather jacket, slight goatee. He's probably mid-twenties.

"Hey, if you ever want to have dinner or something, give me a call. I'm Chad." He hands me his card. I take it as the elevator arrives. "Wait, what's your name?"

"Ella."

"Okay, Ella, call me."

I don't think I want to be an actress anymore. Why work so hard? Any roles I land are prostitutes or sluts. I fell in love with words—Tennessee Williams, Sam Shepard, Shakespeare— words that could live in my body and come out and all I get is "Dance! Dance!" or "Pull out a nose hair." I feel old, like I'm too old for this world that bats me around aimlessly. And I still don't have a job yet. Rent is due soon. The subway platform smells like a mixture of grime and urine. I step on the subway heading downtown, trying to steady myself as the train hurls forward.

* * *

I'm caught inbetween selves, not this one or that one. Michael's girlfriend? An actress? A waitress? I want a fixed identity I can hold onto, I can call mine. My dream was acting, that was everything, but now—

What is all this struggle for? I've hit my wall again and I know the only way to go is down.

The floor is cold in my room. Tears roll down my face—now they come! Where were they when I needed them? The feeling comes again, the heaviness of belonging to nothing. I want to float away from this pain. I can't move—the white ceiling—I can't move—

Someone bangs on my door. "You in there? The phone is for you." It's the DQ.

"Okay, okay, just a sec." I wipe my tears. A miracle? To get me off the floor? The DQ flips her hair back and turns around before I can say thanks. The phone receiver swings from side to side. I catch it. "Hello?"

"Hello, Ella?" It's a man.

"Michael?"

"No, this is Chad."

"Chad?" My brain races back to faces and names.

"Yeah, the camera guy?" Oh, the blond guy with the goatee at the audition.

"How'd you get my number?"

"I have my ways."

There's an awkward silence. Chad jumps in and compliments me for walking out on the audition, that most actresses would never turn down a part. He asks me to meet him at Café de L'Artiste, on 6th avenue. Sure, I'll meet him, he was hot, and a cameraman.

"See you then." I hang up the phone. What am I getting myself into? Oh well, at least it got me off the floor.

NAIL

I spot him in the back of the café, pen in hand sketching something, blond hair, spiked in front. He grins at me.

"There you are." He slides out the chair for me.

"You draw?" The table is round, white, and smooth marble; it's a stark contrast to the dark, warm wooden floor and walls.

"Yes, sometimes." He puts his pencil down.

"That's cool." I take off my blazer and hang it on the back of my chair. He motions the waiter over, a skinny guy with black-rimmed glasses. I order a mocha. I'm nervous, trying to find something to say. His arms are thick and sturdy; I wonder what it would be like sitting on his lap, with those arms around me.

"So, you're a cameraman."

"Yes, that's right."

"Did they cast the part?"

"Another girl—you know, you were the first choice."

"Really? Oh well. Looks like I lost my chance for stardom. Hah."

"You know, there is something special about you." He studies me like I'm a new specimen he's stumbled upon. "Did you know that?" I shrug my shoulders. The waiter places my mocha on the table. He asks how long I've been in the city. My mind scans over my recent flailing about, and I want to lie and provide a glamorous version of my life—but the truth? Too many jobs, too many auditions, too many men . . .

"Almost three years." I take a sip of the mocha.

"Came to make it in the big apple, huh?"

"Yeah, like everyone else. I was in school but dropped out 'cause I couldn't pay for it anymore. I thought, what the heck, I may as well try and make it."

"So, how's it going?"

"You were at my last audition."

"Last?"

"For now. I don't know." Sadness overcomes me. I feel so alone, who has my back? Could he?

He takes my hand. "Let's get out of here." He pays the bill and leads me out of the café into his BMW parked on the street. He swerves in and out of traffic like a seasoned New Yorker. He suggests a movie; sure, that sounds fine.

He parks, opens my door, and helps me out of the car. We sit in the back of the theater; I don't care what movie it is with this man. He puts his arm around me and every so often places his other hand inside my thigh.

I make him drop me off two blocks from the Katherine House. I'm too embarrassed to let him know I live in a women's residence. He double parks the car. "You know, you're exotic, in a good way."

"Good?" I wonder, what is "exotic bad?"

"Yes. What are you?" There it is, the all-too-familiar question.

"Well, I'm mixed."

"With what?"

"Black, American Indian, and Irish."

"Oh." He frowns slightly. "I don't really see the black."

"My grandfather was black." I try and remember my grandfather's face,

"Come here, you're so sexy." He kisses me and runs his hands all over me. "When do I get to see you again?"

"Friday?"

"Okay, Friday it is. I'll call you." I slip out of the car and he drives off.

My mother rarely mentioned my grandfather. I have a faint image of him, a tall man with a deep voice and a big presence.

My brothers and sisters all waited up for him, hoping he would come this time. Many times he said he would come and he didn't, and my mother would say, "I'm sorry your grandfather can't make it." I didn't like the sadness it left in her eyes. The day he came I was five. He looked like the man in the photo posing with the car he made: tall, elegant, handsome, even at his age. "Margaret, Margaret." He embraced my mother and she stepped back a little. I could sense the distance between them. My father, much smaller in stature compared to my grandfather, greeted him with his polite southern accent. "Henry, mighty fine seeing you. How was your trip?"

"Fine, fine, no problem at all." All five of us stood in awe of our grandfather: smooth black skin, large brown eyes, dressed in a smart gray linen suit with a hint of gray in his curly hair.

"Margaret, let me meet your beautiful children." His voice commanded attention. We responded and formed a circle around him as he sat down in the armchair.

"Now, you must be the eldest, Joan, right?" Joan smiled nervously, her black frizzy hair lay tangled against her nightgown. "Hmmm, what do I have for you in my bag, dear?" He displayed a porcelain figure of a horse. "You like horses, don't you?" She nodded shyly and he placed it in her hands.

"Thank you, Grandpa." Joan said. My grandfather playfully tousled her frizzy hair.

"And you, young man, must be Adam, right?" My oldest brother, with his hands in his pockets and head down, every so often dared to peek at him. "Here, I have this belt buckle for you." He handed him a brass buckle of the face of an American Indian. "You're Indian too, remember that. All of you remember that." Grandpa placed his palm on Adam's head. "Don't forget now, who you are."

"I won't," my brother answered, almost inaudibly. "Thank you." He stroked the buckle in his hand.

"And you, curly top, you must be Helen. Helen, come here." He pulled out a fair-skinned doll with jet black curly hair, just like Helen's. She took the doll without saying thank you.

Mom intervened in her calm way. "Now, Helen, say thank

you to your grandfather."

"Thank you," she said quickly and ran off to play with the doll.

"And you, you are Ella. Your hair—Deliah." He whispered the name. "And those eyes." His expression softened. Grandma Deliah. My sister Helen and I would sit with her on the couch and play a game of hiding her cigarettes. She had light skin and reddish hair, and she laughed loud. When she died I cried even though I really never knew her. As if breaking from a trance, my grandfather motioned me over to him. "Pretty Ella, come here. I have a doll as pretty as you." He took out a dark-skinned doll with shiny, straight black hair and bangs framing her plump face. I'd never had a black doll before. "Ella, Ella, always be proud of who you are." The doll's hair shone in the light; she had a stylish blue minidress on.

I held her carefully. "Thank you, Grandpa."

"And last, little Claude. Claude, come here." My little brother wobbled over to him. "Those eyes—like Lloyd's, Margaret, like Lloyd's." He and my mother shared something; the silence told me it was important. "Claude, here, son, a car. Maybe someday you will build a car just like your Grandpa."

"Vrroooom!" Claude shouted in excitement. Grandpa laughed.

"Claude, say thank you to your grandpa," my mother insisted.

Claude mumbled the courtesy and raced his car around the room.

I never played with the doll my grandpa gave me like I played with my white dolls. I made sure she was clean and safe, and placed her on a shelf in a special place where she couldn't be harmed.

* * *

I'm ready, in a tight black minidress, pumps, red lipstick, and short tuxedo jacket. He pulls up in his BMW, double parks, and opens the door for me. "Nice," he says, checking me out.

"Thank you." I flash him a smile. He is dressed New York chic: jeans, black shoes, black V-neck shirt, and his signature spiked blond hair. He's hot. He places his hand on my thigh as he drives, taking it off only to change gears.

"You hungry?"

I want to kiss him all over his face. "Yes."

"Good." The restaurant is chic, a not-too-fancy place in the village. I study the menu. I catch him staring at me and pretend not to notice. His beeper goes off. "Ella, I need to make this call—it's about a job. Can you order for us? I'll take the steak, medium rare."

He walks to the back where the pay phones are and I take this time to apply lipstick. I feel pretty. I think I'm pretty—I suck in my gut. The waiter comes and I order chicken for me, steak for him. Sade plays in the background. I get lost in her voice, singing along.

"Don't stop." He takes his seat. I laugh and blush a little. "Really, you have a nice voice," he says.

I change the subject. "Did you get the job?"

"Yes, I did."

"What is it for?"

"I'll be shooting a music video this week."

"Cool." The waitress serves us, and the food is arranged so artfully, I don't want to touch it. I can barely eat in front of him with the butterflies in my stomach. I get angry at the table that's between us—I want to sit on his lap, let him touch me . . . I manage to get through dinner.

"You want to go to my friend's art show?"

"Sure."

He motions to the waiter, pays the check, and we are out the door.

The curator welcomes us. "You must meet Franz." She is elegant and funky: thigh-high black laced boots, black sequined dress, purple sparkle eye shadow, and fake eyelashes. Her smooth black hair frames her big, brown eyes and red lips—gorgeous. She leads me through the crowd. Chad stops and chats with some friends. Techno music blares, wine glasses clink, smoke lingers in the air. The art is pop abstract installations. People crowd around an installation of plastic bottles, blobs of colorful paint framing the silhouette of a woman's body. Franz wears black like everyone else, except for his orange high top Converse shoes, just to show he is a little different. He is the artist, after all. "Franz, darling, you must meet someone." She steps in front of him, blocking enamored guests hanging on his every word. "This is Chad's new girl." I smile even though the words stick to me: "new girl." A no-name new girl.

"Oh, nice to meet you. Where is Chad?" He dismisses me as if talking to a mannequin. I spot Chad walking towards us with a couple, one clearly a model: tall, blond silky hair, in a black evening dress with a slit up the side. Her man is handsome and tall, built, with brown hair, his arm around her tiny waist. "Ella, great, you've met Franz."

"Sort of . . ."

"These are my friends Eric and Vivien."

I offer my hand before they can say "new girl." "I'm Ella." I shake hands with Eric; Vivien nods at me and smiles. She places her hand on Chad's shoulder.

"Chad and I go back a long time." There is a slight unease in Chad's face.

"Oh really?" I challenge her. "How far?"

"Since high school, right, Chadster? He loves it when you call him that." She moves closer to me and Chad turns and talks with Franz.

"Huh, well, that's good to know."

"So, what do you do, Ella?"

"I do what everyone else does in this town."

"What's that?"

"Chase a dream."

"What dream is that?"

"Acting, and yours?"

"I'm a model."

"Of course." I nod my head.

"Well, it was nice to meet you. Later, Chadster." Chad turns and nods towards her as she hooks arms with Eric, perusing more of the exhibit.

"Chadster?" I nudge him teasingly.

"Don't ask." He takes my arm and leads me out of the gallery. The beat of the techno music follows us out into the street. I'm glad to get out of there away from the tall, perfect, ex-girlfriend model showdown. "Ella, I don't know why she said that, we dated a bit after high school. Nothing serious. Why are you staring at me like that?"

"Like what?"

"Like you can see right through me."

"I'm just looking."

"Don't you know what your eyes can do?"

"No."

"That's the first thing that struck me about you on camera, your eyes. I had to step back, they were so intense. Didn't you know that?"

"No, I didn't."

"Well, you need to be careful with those eyes." He caresses my cheek. I wrap my arms around his neck. "They can pierce a man's soul." His hands rest on my waist.

"Is this okay?" I kiss his whole face—forehead, cheeks, chin, the stubble of his beard, and his lips. We make out like teenagers on the street in the East Village.

His beeper goes off. He checks out the number, says, "Fuck it," and pulls me to him. He asks if I want to come home with him to Brooklyn. Queens and now Brooklyn, what borough is next? Staten Island would be interesting. I try not to be too eager and play it cool—oh forget it, of course I want to be with him.

"Brooklyn, huh?" I playfully bite his lip. He slides his hand down my arm. I take it, and we walk to his car.

The B-52s blare out of his car as we speed across the Brooklyn Bridge, which reminds me of a diamond necklace from a distance. I call it the Diamond Necklace Bridge. He parks at a brownstone under a tree. Inside his place is like a castle, white walls and pillars extending up into high ceilings. He takes me to his bedroom. "I want you, I want you so much." He unzips my dress, kissing my neck, and pulls it over me. We fumble onto his bed. He gets a condom off his nightstand.

"You're beautiful, you know you are beautiful." I let him take me. I dissolve into him and feel myself float away into the white ceiling high above.

We are twisted up in sheets, arms and legs all tangled together. Could I love this man? He gets up and his body is like a Roman statue, something you'd find in a museum, damn. "Stay in bed. I'll make breakfast." He whistles to Aretha Franklin in the kitchen. I fall back to sleep.

The ground is covered with reddish brown leaves. Trees with bare gray branches encircle us. An Indian with long brown hair is with me; I'm not sure who he is. A deer lowers his gray antlers and chews leaves of plants nearby. His round, red back is so close I could touch it. The Indian man says, "Deer walk in circles." The deer lifts his head and moves along the sides of the trees in a circle. A family of deer join him. The stag stops and his back quivers. He transforms into a brown man with black hair, wearing a white tunic and stick antlers on his head. The other deer transform into a family of Indians: children and women in white tunics with the same stick antlers on their heads. They circle around looking for food. The band stops by a white man with a long gray mustache and hat; they extend their cupped palms. He tells them he doesn't have any food but he will get some later. I know he's lying. A young girl with black hair and jet-black eyes offers me something shredded and brown like bark. I take a pinch; it smells sweet. "Oh, tobacco," I say to her. She grins and joins the band.

He gently kisses my forehead. "You okay?" He brushes my lips with his fingers.

"Uh huh." I stretch out my arms and yawn. "Deer, I had a dream about deer."

"Oh yeah?" He traces his fingers on my face. Red brown leaves in a forest, a circle of bare trees, a brown girl offers me something . . .

"Tobacco."

"Huh?"

"A girl gave me tobacco."

"Who?"

"In my dream."

"Hungry?" I suck on his fingers; he lies on top of me. "Breakfast will get cold."

"I don't care."

"There you go, with those eyes again . . ." I smile as he kisses me all over.

The breakfast is cold and we eat it anyways, holding hands and kissing between bites. "So, Ella, what are your plans today?" Chad asks, his round blue eyes like a child's, innocent and open.

"Well, I really should look for a job."

"On Saturday?"

"Rent can't wait."

"Don't worry about that."

"Rent?"

"Let me take you out."

"Where?"

"Central Park."

"Well . . ."

"Come here." I sit on his lap. "You're hot, you know that?" He kisses my neck. "You know that, Ella?" I guess rent can wait.

The lake in Central Park is like a scene from a Monet painting.

Lazy trees hang over the shimmering water, which reflects the sky. We rent a boat; Chad helps me in, and we push off into the lake. Two butterflies dance above us, the constant noise of the city ceases, a dove coos. Just relax, Chad tells me. And for a delicious moment, I do. I allow the boat to rock me. I dip my hand in the cool water and let it swirl around my fingertips.

The night sky is lit up by the fire. She sings a song in the old language as we paddle down the river. I grip the side of the canoe. "Papa! Papa!" We left him in the hole. We left him all alone in the hole. The house fades into the black sky as the canoe drifts around the river bend. I trail my hand in the water. My mama paddles.

The boat bumps against the bank of the lake. It startles me. Chad smiles. "You fell asleep."

"Huh?" I rub my forehead.

"Did you dream?"

"I don't know."

"Ella, what's wrong?" He helps me out of the boat.

"I just didn't want this to end."

"It doesn't have to, Ella, it doesn't have to."

"I'm sorry, Chad, it's just my life is a little fucked up right now."

We walk to his car and I try to gain my composure. He opens the car door for me and helps me in. "You can talk to me, Ella." Tears just keep falling; maybe it is his gentleness that brings them out. I don't have any words; it's a familiar pain that washes over me, a wave I can't control. He double parks the car on my block. "You don't have to go, Ella; you can stay with me. Talk to me, Ella, what's going on?"

"I uh, I'm . . ." I feel weight on my shoulders, the weight of rent due, no job . . .

"Just stay with me, Ella." He strokes my hair. I want to melt into his existence and forget my own, something in me says no.

"I'll call you," I say as I open the door. I get out of his car and walk up the steps to the Katherine House.

* * *

Humpty Dumpty sat on a wall, Humpty Dumpty had a great fall, and all the king's horses and all the king's men couldn't put Humpty together again. I wanted to help Humpty Dumpty, to glue back the pieces of his smashed head, spilled all over the ground. I wanted to help him. I understood him, his brokenness. The camp counselor, a stern-faced young woman, was angry all the time. We went for a long walk in the woods and during the start of the walk I stepped on a board and a nail went right through my blue sneakers, into my foot. I didn't flinch, I didn't make a sound. I just let the nail slide in and out of me as I walked. Each step I took pushed the nail into my foot a little deeper. I didn't stop. I obeyed the rules. I kept walking; it was a long walk.

We got back to the camp and we all were excited to go swimming, taking our shoes and clothes off and changing quickly into our swim suits. I forgot about the nail and the blood on my shoe—I was glad to swim with my friends. The counselor told me to get out of the pool. I followed her to the office. She held my blue sneaker to my face, exposing the bloody nail. "Why didn't you tell us what happened?"

I hunch my shoulders. "I didn't want you to get mad."

She rolled her eyes at her co-worker and got on the phone, calling my daddy.

My father talked with the counselor—they said something about a shot and that I was fine. My father said nothing to me as my brother and sister got in the car and we went home.

I'm still walking with that nail in my foot and I don't know how to stop and take it out. I don't know how, I wish I did, I wish I did.

POOL PARTY

I land another waitress job in the Bowery, a bar next to CBGB's and La MaMa Theatre. It's mostly the theater crowd before and after shows, and of course the regulars. Middle-aged men sit at the bar with rounded stomachs, exchanging sarcastic and witty banter with the bartender and waitstaff. I get to know them. It's an old place; the bar is long, dark wood, the dining area packed with small square tables and curved wooden chairs, something you'd find in a 1920s cabaret. I get to know the chairs intimately, all of them. I close the place three times a week, put chairs up on tables at three in the morning. Nobody bothers me there. I just do my shifts, no groping Joey hands.

Chad picks me up most nights after work. I'm barely at the Katherine House, mostly with Chad and his high white ceilings.

"You sure you need that job?" He strokes my hair with questioning eyes.

"I need it."

"Why? You have me. I can take care of you."

"It makes me get up—"

"What do you mean?" I'm sprawled on the floor reaching for the ties of my black apron 'cause I know it's time to go to work: that's what I mean. I can't say that to him. I shrug my shoulders.

"Think about it." He kisses my forehead. "Come on, get up. We're going to a pool party."

Oh yeah, at his friends' in Long Island. I wonder if model girl will be there—probably. My stomach churns.

It's a modern beach house surrounded by sand and green blades of beach grass. Crows caw angrily at each other in a tree. I wonder what they're saying? It sounds like an argument—Chad pulls me along. "Come on, we're already late."

I squeeze his hand. "Fashionably New York late."

As we walk through the door, the smell of pot and cigarettes greets us. A cacophony of voices and dance music create a dissonant sound, like a chord in a song you wouldn't expect. Thin, scantily-dressed models pose with giraffe-like legs in spiked heels, displaying wine glasses and cigarettes. I feel strangely short and fat, that extra five pounds I'm never able to get rid of—I suck in my gut.

"Chadster!" Vivien glides towards us with Eric trailing behind. She embraces Chad with a fake cheek kiss, careful not to singe his hair with her lit cigarette.

Chad steps back. "You remember Ella?"

"Oh yes, Ella." She gives a fake smile. "Aren't you a nanny or something?"

Chad's face turns red. He lowers his voice and moves closer to her. "Vivien, why would you say that?"

"I'm sorry, she is the spitting image of a nanny I met the other day."

"No. That wasn't me." I fold my arms across my chest.

She turns away, laughing. "Of course not, how silly of me. Ella, come, I'll show you where the powder room is." Before I can protest, she hooks her arm in mine like we're best pals and whisks me to the ladies' room. I try and get Chad's attention but he's talking with his buddy Eric. It's crowded in the powder room with more long-legged women fixing their hair and applying lipstick to already perfect lips.

"Viv!" A thin brunette tosses her sleek hair over her shoulder, kissing Vivien European style. This is getting old. I take my lipstick out of my pocket and smooth it over my lips. A crowd of women surrounds Vivien as she preens in the mirror, carefully administering mascara, answering questions bombarded by the others.

"How's Eric? He looks great!"

"Yes, yes, good, we're good, and what about Sam?" Vivien replies to the thin brunette.

"Oh," the silky-haired brunette pouts, "we broke up, I'm dating someone else."

"Who?"

"Richard, he's my agent."

Another one chimes in. "Vivien, did you get that Jordache ad?" This one is a shadow version of Vivien, blond and frail, like her bones could crack any minute. She casually waits for Vivien's answer as she brushes blush on her protruding cheekbones.

"Oh yes, and it's so exciting. Eric is shooting it!"

"That's so cool!" the shadow Vivien answers.

The brunette chirps, "This is such a great crowd, isn't it? I'm glad there aren't any niggers here."

"Yeah, no kidding," the shadow Vivien agrees. Vivien laughs. I slam my lipstick against the counter and cut off the sound of her cackle.

"Well, there is one here, because I'm black. My grandfather was black, I'm black! Black!" I curl my fists, ready to swing at someone. Heads turn with open mouths and astonished faces.

Vivien gives the perfect exit line. "Let's get something to drink, girls." They snap their compacts and lipstick cases closed, the clicks audible now in the tense silence. Each one brushes past me with slit eyes and raised noses.

Where the hell am I? My body trembles as I walk out and try to find Chad in the crowd. I can't find him, so I begin to drink, one champagne glass after another, until I'm numb, can't feel my anger anymore. A guy offers me a joint. I partake and I am stoned and drunk. I follow the guy to the pool area. What is left for me is delicious water. I take off my dress. I have my bikini underneath, ready to go swimming. The pot guy does a cannonball off the diving board.

I follow him, dizzy from the champagne and pot, and jump into the cool water, my limbs drifting weightless, unencumbered. I submerge, still dizzy, and head towards shallow water. A hand slams my head down. I start to panic and snap out of my drunken state, limbs flailing, trying to escape from arms around my shoulders and hands on my head. Finally, they loosen their grip and let me up. I'm gasping for air, choking. I can make out the girls, the ones in the bathroom, the brunette and two others standing over me as I'm coughing, trying to let in air. "No niggers allowed here," the brunette says. Shadow Vivien laughs, and a shrill cackle follows—Vivien? They hover above me as I make it to the edge of the pool, gasping for air.

Chad comes towards me. "Ella, you okay?"

I try to talk but keep coughing. "I need to go home." Chad helps me out of the water and gets a towel, wraps it around me. "I just need to go home!" I am trembling.

He guides me through the crowd. I walk with my head down, passing through high heels and manicured toes. I am breathing, I can breathe. Chad finds my purse and dress. We stop briefly.

"She okay?" It's Eric.

"Yes, not feeling well. I'm taking her home. See you later, buddy." I wonder if Vivien is there with him, sneering at the soppy mess I've become, or maybe that was her in the pool, holding me down. I start shaking again, I can't stop. Chad heads for the door as fast as he can and we make it outside. I start to vomit in that lovely tall beach grass. He pulls my hair back until I'm done. "Wow, you really can't hold your liquor." I try to stand; my body sways.

"I'm sorry, Chad, I'm sorry." I start puking again.

After I'm done, he gathers me in his arms. "Let's get you home now. I've got to keep an eye on you from now on."

We ride in silence for most of the ride home. Every so often Chad takes my hand and I summon a smile to reassure him I'm alright. But I'm not. Images of the night whirl around my brain; I'm trying to make sense of them. "Chad."

"Yes, honey."

"I don't think your friends like black people."

"Why would you say that?"

"Because some girls, they were gonna drown me or try to,

because they knew I was black."

"What? Ella, you've been drinking too much. Listen, that's ridiculous—how would they even know you were black? You don't even look black."

"I told them. We were in the bathroom, and some of them, I don't know who, jumped me in the pool and held me down."

"No, no, honey, you were drunk, you drank too much."

"They tried to drown me, called me nigger—"

"Ella, honey, shh, shh." He strokes my hair. "My friends would never do that; they're not racist. We're from Manhattan, we work with black people. You just had too much to drink. Everything's gonna be alright, okay?" He strokes my cheek. "I'm taking us home."

Maybe I did make it up—maybe. It was the pot, I was hallucinating, it was like a bad dream; I must have lost balance in the pool. I take in the smell of him, rest my head on his shoulder and fall asleep all the way to Brooklyn. That night he makes love to me hard like he's trying to hold onto me and he needs my body for certainty. "Those eyes, Ella, what are behind those eyes?" I trace his lips. "You're mine, aren't you mine, Ella?" His want makes me alive.

"Yes, I'm yours, I'm yours." And he comes and I lay my head on his chest. I let myself sink into the warmth of his arms and he cradles me. He kisses my forehead.

"Ella, I want you to meet my parents." Uh oh, I'm barely making it through meeting his friends—

I nuzzle my head underneath his arm and fall asleep.

I'm sweating I can't breathe, feel suffocated gasping for air. "Chad! Chad!"

"They were holding me down, they were . . ." My heart is racing.

"Ella, you just drank too much, shh, baby, I'm here."

"Chad, they were trying to drown me—"

"Sweetie, my friends would never do that. Here, let me get you something to help you sleep." He gets up, goes in the bathroom and comes back with two white pills and a glass of water. I swallow each pill. He tells me not to worry, that they're just jealous, that's all. The pills take their effect and within minutes I am knocked out.

My head is pounding. Chad is getting ready for a video shoot. What day is it? Do I have to work tonight? My head throbs in my hands.

"That bad, huh?" He kisses my cheek. "I've got to go in a few; here's cab money to get home."

"Oh, I can take the subway."

He lets out an exasperated sigh. "Please, take a cab, sweetie. I don't want to worry."

"The subway station is right around the block—"

"Promise me you'll take a cab?"

"Okay." He kisses me one last time and heads out the door. It's quiet in here without him. The high white ceilings, white sheets, everything elegant and artsy: just like Chad. Images of last night rush in my head: high heels, long legs, ruby lips, and me talking about my grandfather, my black grandfather. The exodus out of the bathroom, sneers in the mirror. It did happen, right? Right? I start to feel panicky again, try and push the feelings down—I was drunk, high, and they were just jealous of me like Chad said, jealous. After a shower, I put myself together carefully: hair, lipstick, Walkman, sunglasses. I leave the cash Chad left me on the table and decide to take the subway instead.

I'm a dot in the commute crowd, among many hundreds of dots feeding the subway turnstile—how will we all get through? I feel the tiredness of the crowd, the resignation of the nine to five work week. My head's in a blur.

* * *

We all fight for the window seat. Until Dad stomps down the wooden steps to the garage—then we get quiet. We know better than to bicker in front of him. My mother's gentle footsteps trail behind him. She is solemn, her large eyes sadder than usual as we pile into the gray station wagon and head north to Maine for her father's funeral. Since Claude and I are the youngest and smallest we have to sit in the far back in makeshift seats. I feel cheated because I'm ten, almost a teen. Joan, Adam, and Helen sit in the back seats and my parents sit up front. Dad drives. Classical music plays softly on the radio. My parents argue. As usual, my Dad is worried about the time and angry at my mother's habitual lateness. My mother tells him to calm down. Tension permeates the car.

The church is in a modest neighborhood. It's hot and muggy as we walk up the steps in silence. A woman dressed in black with a large hat greets us; her skin is coffee brown and she is large boned like my mother.

"Aunt Beah!" My mother embraces her as we all stand around them.

"Little Margaret. Oh, and your brood! Deliah would have been glad you all made it."

"Yes, yes, she would have been. Aunt Beah, these are my children and this is R.J." We all smile and nod, and my father offers his hand.

"Pleased to meet you."

"Yes. Well, here are programs and you all better go in, it already started." Mom and Dad lead the way down the aisle. Proud afros of every size fill the pews like halos. As we walk to our seats in the front, heads turn with scrutiny like we are a misplaced family at the wrong funeral. Aunt Beah joins us and sits next to Mom. The casket is regal, shiny purple. It's open, and I can make out my grandfather's profile. Mom told me he had lots of wives, four to be exact. I turn around: all the black people with the Jackson 5 afros are my relatives. I've never met them. I only met my grandfather once before, and now he's dead.

At the end of the sermon we all stand in line and wait to view the body. The organ music swells as we step slowly in a long line that winds around the church snake-like.

"Henry, Henry, all these people are here for you, just you."

"Deliah, Deliah—"

"I'm here for you baby, I waited for you, just like I said I would, baby—"

"Deliah, my delight . . ."

"Yes, darling, yes . . ."

A woman breaks out in sobs as she crumples over his body. "Henry! Oh, my Henry!" Grasping a tissue, she wails. Another woman gently leads her past the coffin. "Priscilla, come on now, he's in the Lord's hands now, come on."

"That's Priscilla, my wife, Priscilla. Deliah, she's calling me!"

"Baby, I'm right here, shh, shh."

"I need to go to her!"

"Come here, baby, I'm right here, come here."

"They can't hear us."

"No, they can't."

"I can't go back?"

"No, you can't."

"Deliah?"

"Yes?"

"Hold me, hold me, Deliah."

"Yes, baby, yes."

In the casket, my grandfather's chocolate brown skin glistens against purple satin. His eyes are closed, he can't see me. This is how I will remember him, impeccably dressed in a black suit, and I can't see his eyes, can't see his eyes.

I'm glad to get out of the church. People gather in groups and my family forms a small circle. No one talks. My mother's Aunt Beah joins us with a tall black man who approaches my mom.

"Margaret." My mother turns and a warm smile spreads

across her face.

"Kenny." She embraces him. My mother introduces us to our Uncle Kenny and we shyly shake his hand. "Where's Hank and Sammy?" my mother asks Uncle Kenny.

"They're at Priscilla's already." His voice is soft and low like a double bass.

"Oh, we will meet them there," my mother responds. There's a knowing silence between them. A large shadow cast over us. I point to the sky. All heads turn up to a majestic wingspan.

"What kind of bird is that?" Claude asks.

"Why, I believe that is a bald eagle. What on earth is a bald eagle doing over here?" my father says incredulously.

"Maybe it's hungry," Joan adds. Soon the whole crowd outside the church cranes their necks to view the grand eagle.

"It's a sign," Aunt Beah says.

"A sign of what?" my mother asks.

"Emma is visiting us." She places her hand on her chest.

"Who's Emma?" I ask.

"Emma is your great-grandmother, my mother. She was Indian and black."

"And now she's an eagle?" Claude jokes. My brothers and sisters try to stifle their laughter.

"Yes, she is giving us a message," Aunt Beah whispers.

My father shakes his head. The eagle descends one more time towards us and sails above the clouds.

"That was a rare sighting, that eagle, extremely rare. What are the odds of that?" Dad leads the way to the station wagon; we get in the car and head to Priscilla's house.

Every house has the same layout: one level, with a square patch of grass in front yellowing from the August sun. My father pulls into the driveway. A few men smoke cigarettes, R&B music blares from the open door. I smell pot. As we pile out of the car the woman who broke down in front of the casket gives the same performance as she enters the door.

"OHHHH, my Henry's gone!" She slouches forward, catches her hat so it doesn't fall. People gather around her and prop her up as she weeps uncontrollably. I have never experienced this kind of display of emotion in my life. In our house, it's hush, hush, don't say a word, especially if you're sad, go away and hide. I want to scream and cry like her. I want to be held too. We all stand awkwardly on the yellowed lawn, my mother talking with Uncle Kenny and a skinny black man with a big smile. He turns to my mother.

"Margaret, you've done well!" He has a jovial demeanor, quite different from Uncle Kenny's.

"Oh, Sammy!" My mother smiles and introduces us all to Uncle Sammy.

"So, which one of you wants to go for a ride on my scooter?" He points to a blue and white scooter bike parked on the sidewalk. No one answers so I say I'll go.

I get on the back of the scooter bike, he tells me to hold onto his waist, and we speed off. The wind makes my eyes water a bit, makes my hair flow back, as we speed up and down blocks while Sammy greets people, beeping his horn, announcing: "Hey you all! This is my niece! Say hi to my niece!" I wave and people smile and wave back from their porches. Sammy zooms down another block. I giggle, holding onto this man I just met, my Uncle Sammy, and I feel like a movie star.

Uncle Sammy turns into the driveway and parks his scooter on the side of the road. I thank him. In the yard a skinny man with an afro has a cigarette in one hand and a beer in the other, talking loudly to my mother. He sways a bit back and forth and slurs his words. "Margaret, Margaret, you got out, didn't you! Out! I missed you, but I was glad, I am glad, everyone drink to Margaret for getting out!" He takes a swig of his beer. My mom puts her hand on his shoulder, trying to calm him.

"He did nothing for us, Margaret, you remember? Nothing. We begged for food, he left us with nothing, remember, Margaret?

Remember . . . ? He was no father. NO FATHER!"

"I know, Hank, I know." My mom places her hand on his back.

"Margaret, he left us with that crazy woman, you know, and you know who got the worst of it. You know, Francine. She's locked up! Did you know that? Aw, Margaret, you got out, you got out, I'm so glad you got out!" He's kneeling on the lawn; my mother has her arms around him trying to get him to stand. Francine, that's her sister that calls mom every so often. I overheard a conversation and mom was telling her to let it go, it was in the past, that mother is dead now. She was flustered when she got off the phone. Where is Francine locked up? Why can't we visit her?

"Shh, Hank, that was a long time ago. Let it go, Hank." And she helps him to his feet.

"Margaret, maybe I'll get out too, one day."

Uncle Sammy puts his arm around him. "Come on, brother, let's get you home."

"Sammy, you know what? If I could stop drinking, if I could, but this here bottle here has got me wrapped up, wrapped up hard! It's the Irish in me, right, Margaret?" He takes another swig, laughing. He breaks free from Uncle Sammy's embrace and steps up to my father, who is trying to herd us all into the car. "Now you all come back soon again. I mean it, you all are welcome here."

"Okay, that's mighty nice, now everyone get in the car," my father frowns.

"Really, really welcome." He starts to sway again like he's going to fall smack on my father, Uncle Kenny steadies him.

"Now come on, Hank, it's time to get you home," Uncle Kenny says calmly.

"Sammy, I mean Kenny, those are our nephews and nieces, you know? Right there. Isn't that something?" Hank smiles at us as we wait in the car for Mom.

"Yes, Hank, now come on." Uncle Kenny is trying to guide

him away from the car.

"You all be sure to come back soon!" My father ignores him, gets in the car, slams the door and honks the horn. My mother stands in front of her brother Hank and puts her hand on his cheek.

"Now Hank, you take care of yourself, alright?"

"Margaret, one day I'll get out, you'll see."

"Yes, Hank, yes." He takes her hand, then lets it go. Uncle Sammy and Uncle Kenny prop him up as we back out of the driveway to go home.

"Astor Place," the driver announces. I'm jostled awake as the crowd piles out of the open doors. Startled, I get up, and they push me along with them like a herd of sheep. Where am I? Oh yeah, Astor Place. I must have passed out. I head west down 8th Street, my head still pounding, limbs heavy. The heat of the day hasn't crept over the city yet. The sun waits menacingly, ready to press the air between the buildings, making it unbearable like a sauna. Something familiar creeps inside me, the unnamable sadness.

I feel tears in my throat, why? I need to get home to the Katherine House, get ready for my shift at work. I start to panic as the sepulchral heaviness overwhelms me. I make it home, to my room, the cold linoleum floor. And I break down.

Hands over my head in the pool. Did it happen? Did it? My chest heaves. Chad's voice comes into my head. "You just drank too much. My friends would never do that." I want it to stop, I want the pain to stop—

This pain that follows me wherever I go, finds me no matter what, wrestles me to the ground. How long can I exist like this? This fall-down-get-up dance? How long? I need something to stop this pain—to feel another pain—to end this pain to—

I need to get ready for work. I reach for my apron strings on the floor and get up.

At work I hover above myself, trying to keep up the pace of the rush hour, happy hour. Hah, why not call it despair hour? Disgruntled customers with impatient faces, unforgiving faces. "I said a martini on the rocks!" A skinny white man with thick, black-rimmed glasses reprimands me. He tells his friend, talking loud enough so I can hear, "That girl should not be a waitress, she should go back to acting." And they both laugh. I pretend not to hear and somehow get through my shift. Not bad, not bad, seventy bucks. Considering my state, I call it a success.

Chad is picking me up to meet his parents. I quickly go to the bathroom, change my shirt, redo my lipstick, eyeliner, spray some Ralph Lauren perfume to combat the bar stench and wait for him at the bar. A regular comes in with a tiny gray kitten. "Hey, guys, check this out." He plops the kitten on the bar. Rough hands grope at the poor thing; it's terrified.

"Where'd you get this?" the bartender asks.

"It just came to me on the street." The kitten shivers on the bar. I want to take her away from the loud voices, rough hands, tuck her in my shirt and run. Pure innocence that kitten, pure— and I spot Chad's BMW and run out to meet him.

"Hey, beautiful!"

"Hey." We kiss.

"We're meeting my parents for dinner."

"I know."

"You're wearing that?"

"What's wrong with this?" He's never questioned my East Village street-fashion style before.

"My parents, well, they would expect you in something nicer—not that you don't look nice—just dressier." I think of all my clothes and can't summon up anything that's dressy.

"Chad, I don't have anything."

"Don't worry, I know where to go." We head uptown. "We'll get you something, we have time." We end up at Bloomingdale's, the one near Jan's. I almost want to stop in there, then I remember

I told the manager to fuck off. Not a good idea. "Come on, come on." Chad hurries me along; we take the escalator to the women's department. The bright lights and all the clothes make me feel dizzy: too many choices. He picks out a black fitted dress with a white belt, the kind of outfit a newscaster or politician's wife would wear. I frown. "Just for tonight, Ella, wear it just for tonight." I oblige and try it on in the dressing room. I suck in my gut and step out to show Chad. "There's my girl," he says, smiling. He buys the dress. I wear it out of the store and bundle my rejected clothes under my arm. Chad, in a blazer, white button-down shirt, and jeans, and I in that trophy-wife dress glide out of Bloomingdale's like two store mannequins come to life: what a picture.

The doorman greets us as he opens the heavy ornate door.

We walk to the elevator. Inside, Chad presses the button to the eighth floor. "Come here, gorgeous." He runs his hands up and down my dress, kissing my neck.

I giggle. "Chad, stop!" Not really meaning it. We get to the eighth floor. I straighten my dress out and Chad pats me on the bottom. I playfully punch his arm, smiling.

He knocks on the door. A striking, middle-aged woman with black hair opens the door, smiles. Chad introduces me. "Ella, this is my mother, Adrienne."

"Hello." I offer her my hand. She skillfully sizes me up, a slight disdain in her eyes. Dress not up to her standards?

"Very pleased to meet you, Ella." She drops my hand; her lips form a straight line. I sense she will just tolerate my presence in her home. She motions us to the living room: expensive art dominates the walls, plush carpet on the floor, along with a breathtaking view of the city. Chad's father walks towards me with a martini glass in his hand. He's tall with thinning salt and pepper hair, parted on the side to hide a bald spot. His eyes are like Chad's: watery blue, large, and round.

"You must be Ella, pleased to meet you. I'm Bob." I smile

and shake his hand. "Ella, please sit down." I feel strangely grateful to Chad that he bought me this dress that fits into the setting
of this upscale Eastside apartment. I plant a smile on my face
and obediently wait for Chad for the next cue. He hands me a
drink, vodka and tonic, sits down, and places his hand on my
thigh. Adrienne casts her eyes towards me. Is that a glimmer of
disapproval? Or is that disgust? Chad doesn't remove his hand.
I blush.

"So, Ella." Adrienne takes a sip of her drink, reclines on the
couch. "Chad tells me you are from New England."

"Yes, Boston area, a small town."

"Well, what brings you to New York?"

"I went to school here, for a while."

"And what did you study?"

"Theater."

"And what do you do now?"

"Right now, I'm waitressing."

"Of course. Chad went through that phase of wanting to be
an actor. Didn't you, honey? It's a tough business." She places her
drink on the table. "Have you seen his work?"

"No, I haven't, he hasn't shown it to me." I put my hand on
his thigh.

"Come on, Mother, you're embarrassing me." Chad takes a
long sip of his drink.

"Well, you were very good."

"You're just saying that because you're my mother."

"I'm saying that because I know. After all, I am a casting
director." She slightly lifts her chin in the air, staring at me like
a queen in a chess game waiting for the right move. Am I the
pawn?

I turn to Chad's father. "Are you in the same business as
well?"

"No, no, nothing exciting like that. I do marketing for
Chevron."

"Well, it's about time for dinner," Adrienne announces. Chad leads me into the dining room, pulls out my chair, and scoots me in at the table. "Chad, honey, would you please serve the plates?"

"Sure." He places a plate of white fish, rice, and green beans in front of me.

"So, Ella, what are your plans?"

"Plans?" I feel flushed again.

"Yes, now that you are no longer in college."

"Well, I'm an actress."

"So that's your plan?"

"Yes, for now."

"I guess it's a good time for your type—ethnics are quite in these days."

"Really?" Bob says, surprised.

"Yes, I've noticed it in commercials, a greater need for ethnic types, quite a surge. Someone like Ella is much more sought after now than, let's say, ten years ago," Adrienne continues. "It's definitely not Ozzie and Harriet any more, is it?" She laughs.

"No, it's not." Bob chuckles in response.

"Those were the good old days: things were much simpler," Adrienne says wistfully, emphasizing the word "simpler."

"Ella and I met during an audition," Chad chimes in, squeezing my thigh.

"Oh, for what?" Adrienne feigns interest.

"That B movie I told you about?"

"Oh yes, now I recall. And did Ella get the part?"

I don't know whether to answer or not. I don't know if I am in the conversation. They seem to have dissolved me; I am only necessary as some prop that can't talk. My throat constricts. I finish my drink.

"Ella walked out of the audition."

"She did? Why?"

"She didn't like the script. That's how she got my attention."

Chad turns to me and kisses me. At this point I have no words. I am just a body and he is my spokesperson.

"How unusual, Ella, to walk out." Adrienne slightly raises her eyebrows.

"Yes, unusual," Bob agrees.

"I was just playing hard to get." I break through the silence and Bob and Adrienne laugh.

Chad whispers in my ear, "Well, it worked for me."

Thankfully, the dinner is almost over. Something is choking inside me and I don't let it show. I perform the required good-bye rituals, smiles and handshakes, and Chad and I leave the apartment, down to his car and to Brooklyn.

He unzips my dress in the hallway. "I want you. I've wanted you all night." My body is rigid and he stops kissing my neck. "Babe, what's wrong?"

"I don't think your parents like me."

"Nonsense, why would you think that?'

"I just got that feeling . . ."

"Of course they like you. Who wouldn't like you? You're wonderful!" He pulls down my dress and carries me to his bed.

A streetlight glows through the window. My mind won't stop. Chad's mother, her hatred leaked through her eyes—but Chad said they liked me—I'm wonderful. I made them laugh— I'm wonderful—the ethnic type—I'm wonderful—pull off my dress—fuck me—I'm wonderful—

this paper doll this cut-out version of—

where am I?

And I begin to crack and something is unleashed—

and my tears won't stop.

The bathroom floor is cold. I float above myself. Will I fall? Will I crack into a thousand pieces?

Humpty Dumpty sat on a wall Humpty Dumpty had a great fall—

He came after me. I ran through the house up the stairs as fast as I could go got on the top of the bunk bed where he couldn't get me. His hands caught my pant leg and pulled me down crashing on the floor he pulled off my pants his weight on me a knife through my belly I can't move knife feels like a knife between my legs, something wet slippery, the light, white glass, with designs on it like a snowflake a flower a flower snowflake—

"No niggers allowed here." *I can't breathe—*

"You're mine, aren't you mine, Ella?"

Who's gonna put me back together? All the pieces I have become?

The light in Chad's bathroom flickers. How do I stop the pain stop it stop it—*Wait till I get your brothers. He leaves me to get my brothers I am broken—*

How do I stop this pain. I grab a razor—

"Honey." Chad knocks on the door. "You in there?'

It's too late. "Ella!" He comes in. "Ella!"

"I just wanted it to stop the pain to stop stop . . ." He gets a towel and takes the razor out of my hand.

"What the fuck, Ella! Why'd you do this?" He wraps my wrist in a towel.

"I wanted it to stop."

"Stop what, Ella? Ella, we gotta get you—let me think, we gotta go."

He squeezes my wrist as he drives; it's bleeding through the towel. Over the Diamond Necklace Bridge into Manhattan to a white building on the East Side. "Bellevue."

"Ha, this is the only time I'll get to play Blanche DuBois."

"What?" He slams on the brakes, almost hitting the car in front of us.

"*A Streetcar Named Desire.* Blanche DuBois, the scene at the end when they take her away."

"Ella, this is no play, this is real life."

"I know, but think about it, when would I, the 'ethnic' type, ever be cast as Blanche?"

"What the hell are you talking about? Jesus Christ! You could bleed to death!" He parks the car and walks me through the emergency doors. A nurse greets us with a clipboard, taking down information. She takes me in a room and bandages my wrist. Chad waits in the waiting room. It's not too crowded; I suppose they needed to take me first, because of the bleeding. The nurse places a plastic hospital bracelet around my wrist and sends me back to the waiting room. Chad whispers with the nurse. I feel strangely calm, like I've stopped fighting—I've finally surrendered to this war inside. Chad walks over to me with a clipboard in his hands and touches my shoulder. "Honey, you need to sign this, so they can help you." He hands me the clipboard and I scribble my signature with my good hand. He returns the clipboard to the desk. "I'm going to go now." He has tears in his eyes. I want to shout, *"No, don't leave me, don't leave me, Chad."* I can't. I have stepped over the sane line to the other side of sanity.

"Thank you," I say meekly, trying to smile—I break down, collapse to the floor, and the intake guy, a tall black man with gentle eyes, puts his hand on my back, and tenderly lifts me up. I smile at him; I can't resist—I recite in a perfect Southern accent: "I have always depended on the kindness of strangers." Blanche DuBois's famous line as she exits the scene gracefully and the two men come to take her away to the funny farm. And I'm laughing and crying simultaneously. The intake man takes my elbow.

Chad tries to console me. "Ella, it's going to be okay. I'll check on you tomorrow."

I can't bear to meet his eyes. Chad, I'm so sorry, I didn't mean to fall apart at the seams—didn't mean to. Come on, get ahold of yourself, Ella, wait—I'm in Bellevue, I don't have to.

The intake guy leads me to another waiting room, smaller, in front of a large wooden door bearing an official brass-plated sign, "Dr. Simon, Psychiatrist" in black letters. "Wait here, the doctor will meet with you shortly." The tone of his voice soothes me; I feel instantly grateful for his kindness.

I sit in a hard, plastic white chair in front of a window. It's raining; droplets form on the glass. My wrist throbs. I feel the pain now, pain I caused myself to stop pain. I am broken, a broken toy Chad dropped off, doesn't work anymore—take it back take it back.

The door opens and a blond lady appears, young, with bangs and round glasses like John Lennon's. How's this white lady gonna help me? She gestures me to sit on a padded chair across from her impressive desk, where she sits and appears even smaller, more childish, like she was playing doctor. Or shrink. "So, tell me, Ella," she says in a clipped, superior tone as she arranges papers in front of her, "what brings you here?"

"Just trying to beat the holiday crowd."

She tilts her head, purses her lips, and asks in a serious tone, "Yes, continue, what about the holidays?" Her pen is perched above her paper, ready to strike at any time. I'm disappointed she didn't get my joke.

"It's September. Soon the stores will tell us it's Halloween, they'll clear the merchandise for Thanksgiving, Christmas, there is no time. So, I just figure I better squeeze my breakdown in there somewhere." Once I explain it, I realize it's not funny. She pauses as if deeply concerned. I break the silence. "I was joking." Wow, I have to spell it out for her.

"This is no joke. Because you cut yourself, didn't you, Ella?"

My bandaged wrist stings. "Yes. I did."

"And why, do you know why you cut yourself?" She sounds affected, like she's a talk show host addressing a contestant on *Why Did You Try and Kill Yourself?* She raises her pen in the air expectantly.

The cold floor the glass light with flower snowflake the searing pain between my legs

I can't breathe they're holding me down, Chad, they tried to drown me, Chad—

"Ethnic types are in now, aren't they?"

Tears run down my face, words are caught in my throat, I can't speak.

"We can help you, Ella." I try to appear stoic, in control. "Although we do not have any beds right now, we can set up a cot in the hallway for you."

Wait. Beds, hallway, overnight? I snap back into reality, into the moment.

"Overnight? I can't. I have to work tomorrow."

"Your boyfriend signed you in, and you signed the papers."

"What?"

"That means, as long as you are a danger to yourself or others, we can keep you for seventy-two hours."

"But I have to work tomorrow—"

"We can help you."

"I can't lose my job! How is that helping me?" I panic and run to the door. "I've got to get out of here!" She pushes a red button on the wall.

"Ella, Ella, calm down, we can help you." Two nurses appear at the door, one man and one woman with stern faces. "Please set a cot up for Ella in the hallway and make sure she takes these meds." She hands the male nurse a slip of paper.

"I can't stay here, please, I have to work tomorrow!" I try and move past them; the nurses take ahold of my arms and lead me down the hall. The doctor's clipped tone, "Next," reverberates in the hallway. The woman nurse is middle-aged with tired eyes. She hands me a small white cup with two pills in it and a cup of water.

"Take these," she says. The male nurse towers over me.

"What is it?" I ask, aware that the male nurse is close by, just in case I refuse.

"It will calm you down, make you feel better." She turns her wrist and glances at her watch. I bet she can't wait until work is over. I take a pill, put it in my mouth and take a swig of water, pretending to swallow, and do the same with the second one. I hand the nurse the empty white cup. "Done?" she asks. I nod to her, trying to keep the pills under my tongue. I can taste their bitterness. I stop at the bathroom and the nurse lets me go in alone. I close the door, spit the pills in the toilet, and flush them down. The nurse guards escort me to a hallway and set up a cot near a light-skinned black woman with disheveled hair, pacing, mumbling to herself, unaware of our presence.

"They never let you out of here, they never let you leave, they never let you out, they never let you leave . . ." The nurse guards hand me a blanket and tell me this is my cot. Muffled screams penetrate the hallway. How am I gonna get out of here? I start to panic, my heart races, the sobs I can't stop—

"Whose baby are you?" A black woman with a beautiful round face and almond eyes, eyes like mine but bigger, beams down at me.

"Huh?" I try to stifle my crying. How did she get here? I hadn't seen her before. Maybe a new patient.

"Never mind, chile. You got to get yourself together." Something in her voice makes me listen, a certainty. "Now, you didn't swallow any pills, did you?" I shake my head. "Good. Good." She sits down. "Now listen, chile, you better find out who you are before they take you and you forget everything. Feel the ground, the earth. You're strong you know, you got ancestors you know, they're here. You're strong enough to stand and feel them, I can tell. Get up now and do what I tell you so you can get on out of here." Her words rush over me like cold water waking me up from some kind of sleep I was in but didn't know it.

Black curls frame her face and almond eyes. I ask her name.

"Julia, you can call me Julia," she says.

"I'm Ella."

"Now get yourself together, girl, the more you fall apart around here, the longer you'll stay."

"How long have you been here?"

"Oh, I'm getting out in a few days."

"You see ancestors?"

"They've been waiting for you, Ella, for you to wake up and listen." With that, Julia stands up, says goodnight, and heads towards the distressed woman pacing in the hall.

"Good night and thank you." I fall asleep and feel somehow protected.

That night I dreamt I was at the edge of the ocean and a great big porpoise leaped out of the water, spraying me. I walked farther down the beach and Chad was there with a group of friends, laughing and drinking. I tried to get Chad's attention and tell him about the giant porpoise but he couldn't see or hear me. I sat down on a large rock. A dark Indian girl basked in the sun on a wide, flat rock. She rose slowly and spread out her arms. Feathers sprouted out of her limbs, face, and body and she soared to the sky. The rock lit up in the sunlight, revealing drawings etched on its surface. I rubbed my fingers over the figures of birdlike men and animals. A red salamander crawled on top of the stone. I picked it up and swallowed it.

Sunlight streaks through the hall. I rub my eyes, forgetting where I am. A pit forms in the bottom of my belly. Oh yeah, the hospital. What a dream I had last night—are these the ancestors Julia is talking about? I want to ask her, I don't see her anywhere. I get up and her words ring in my ears: "Keep yourself together."

Three days pass. I continue to pretend to swallow my pills and keep myself intact. Chad doesn't visit me. I guess it's over. I just need to focus on getting out of here. It's almost my turn to meet with the doctor. This is my exit performance, the "I'm well enough to leave" act. I plan on giving the Academy Award-winning performance of my life. The doctor opens her door. "Ella, how are you?" She puts down her papers.

"I'm well."

"Have you had any more suicidal thoughts?"

"No, no, in fact I feel a lot better. I'm ready to go back to my life, back to work."

"It's been a short time here for you. I want to make sure you don't slip through the cracks." She looks at me like I am going to fall right now through a crack in the floor. She wants to make sure they haven't missed anything. She wants to observe me for a bit longer. Hell no, longer? I want to shout, turn over her desk and wipe the smug expression off her face. I don't—something comes over me and I channel Lauren Bacall, or Katherine Hepburn, or both of them at the same time,

"Doctor, I assure you that is not necessary. I've missed far too much work and really want to get back to my life. This has helped me and I thank you for your help. I know I have gotten what I need." I almost slip into a British accent.

"Hmmmmm." She pauses. "I'm going to refer you to our outpatient clinic, however you must sign this document stating you will continue care there." I feel the panic leave me. Outpatient. Anything is better than staying here another minute. The doctor hands me the document and I sign it quickly. She wishes me good luck and I thank her, ending the performance with my best fake smile.

Julia is waiting in the hall. "I'm leaving," I say.

"I told you."

"Is this your last day too?"

"Yes, I'll be gone, I'll be gone."

"Thank you, Julia . . ."

Julia places her palms on my cheeks, cradling my head. "Just remember, Ella, once you let someone define you—you die." She releases her hands, glances at me one last time, and enters the doctor's office.

I walk out that door into the sunshine, rip off the plastic bracelet, and head down the street with words, words I can stand on.

ACKNOWLEDGEMENTS

These characters have been haunting me for years. I sat down at my kitchen table for six years and let them speak. Thank you, dear reader, for picking up this book and allowing them to come to life. I wish to express deep gratitude to the following first readers for their inspiring words and support: Jerry Thompson, Andy Weiner, Lucille Lang Day, Roberta Lee Tennant, Abby Abinanti, Nanette Deetz, and Chris Lombardi. Many thanks to Kirsten Johanna Allen for bearing witness to my work with her profound insight and expertise and all the talented staff at Torrey House Press: Kathleen Metcalf, Mark Bailey, Rachel Davis, Brooke Larsen, and Anne Terashima. I am so honored to include Lucille Clifton's poem; many thanks to Jerry Thompson for facilitating the permissions, Lucille Clifton's family, and Rachel Davis. Special thanks to my sister Lisa Terrell for sharing her knowledge about our ancestors, and Elaine Dennis, Liz McCarthy, Olivia Dempster, and Robin Greenberg for their ongoing support. Works in Progress has been an invaluable group where I was able to share the first scenes of my novel; thank you, Linda Zeiser and Carolyn Zeiser, for facilitating this safe creative space for women artists. Lastly, thanks to the hummingbirds, ocean, rivers, and the earth, to my ancestors and their untold stories, may they be released and healed.

Woliwon.

ABOUT ALISON HART

Alison Hart studied theater at New York University and later found her voice as a writer. She identifies as a mixed-race African American, Passamaquoddy Native American, Irish, Scottish, and English woman of color. Her poetry collection *Temp Words* was published by Cosmo Press in 2015, and her poems appear in *Red Indian Road West: Native American Poetry from California* (Scarlet Tanager Books, 2016) and elsewhere. Hart lives in Alameda, California.

TORREY HOUSE PRESS

Voices for the Land

The economy is a wholly owned subsidiary of the environment, not the other way around.

—Senator Gaylord Nelson, founder of Earth Day

Torrey House Press is an independent nonprofit publisher promoting environmental conservation through literature. We believe that culture is changed through conversation and that lively, contemporary literature is the cutting edge of social change. We strive to identify exceptional writers, nurture their work, and engage the widest possible audience; to publish diverse voices with transformative stories that illuminate important facets of our ever-changing planet; to develop literary resources for the conservation movement, educating and entertaining readers, inspiring action.

Visit www.torreyhouse.org for reading group discussion guides, author interviews, and more.

As a 501(c)(3) nonprofit publisher, our work is made possible by the generous donations of readers like you. Join the Torrey House Press family and give today at www.torreyhouse.org/give.